D1058397

from

THE MAKING OF AMERICANS

from THE MAKING OF AMERICANS

gleanings from the book by

GERTRUDE STEIN

edited by D. Sorensen

MUNKLINDE VESTERGAARD
Nambe, New Mexico

Endpapers and additional drawings by Mina Yamashita

The editor is grateful to Calman A. Levin and the Estate of
Gertrude Stein for permission to quote from one of Stein's letters
to Sherwood Anderson, originally printed in "The Making of *The
Making of Americans*", by Donald Gallup, and reprinted in *Fernhurst,
Q.E.D. and Other Early Writings*, by Gertrude Stein.

Library of Congress Cataloging-in-Publication Data

Stein, Gertrude, 1874-1946
    From The making of Americans : gleanings from the book by
Gertrude Stein / edited by D. Sorensen.
        p.   cm.
    Abridged ed. of : The making of Americans
    ISBN 0-9640280-1-8
    1. Family--United States--Fiction.
I. Sorensen, D. (Douglas)   II. Stein, Gertrude, 1874-1946.
Making of Americans.   III. Title.
PS3537.T323M33 1994
813'.52--dc20   94-4184

Printed in the United States of America
1 3 5 7 9 0 8 6 4 2

This version of
The Making of Americans
is for
Alfred Hersland and Julia Dehning

It began with Conrad Skinner's
question and would never have got
done or would have got poorly done
without Mina Yamashita's lore and
Jeff Lawrence's ear. *Tusind tak.*

Contents

from

THE MAKING OF AMERICANS

Once an angry man dragged his father along the ground through his own orchard. "Stop!" cried the groaning old man at last, "Stop! I did not drag my father beyond this tree."

It is hard living down the tempers we are born with. We all begin well, for in our youth there is nothing we are more intolerant of than our own sins writ large in others and we fight them fiercely in ourselves; but we grow old and we see that these our sins are of all sins the really harmless ones to own, nay that they give a charm to any character, and so our struggle with them dies away.

It has always seemed to me a rare privilege, this, of being an American, a real American, one whose tradition it has taken scarcely sixty years to create. We need only realize our parents, remember our grandparents and know ourselves and our history is complete.

The old people in the new world, the new made out of the old, that is the story that I mean to tell, for that is what really is and what I really know.

We, living now, are always to ourselves young men and women. When we, living always in such feeling, think back to them who make for us a beginning, it is always as grown and old men and women or as little children that we feel them, they whose lives we have just been thinking. We sometimes talk it long, but really, it is only very little time we feel ourselves ever to have being as old men and women or as children. Such parts of our living are never really there to us as present, to our feeling.

Yes we are very little children when we first begin to be to ourselves grown men and women. We say then, yes we are children, but we know then, way inside us, we are not to ourselves real as children, we are grown to ourselves, as young grown men and women. Very little things we are then and very full of such feeling. And so it is to be really old to ourselves in our feeling; we are weary and are old, and we know it in our working and our thinking, and we talk it long, and we can see it just by looking, and yet we are a very little time really old to ourselves in our feeling, old as old men and old women once were and still are to our feeling. No it must be always as grown and young men and women that we know ourselves and our friends in our feeling. To be ourself like an old man or an old woman to our feeling must be a horrid losing-self sense to be having.

Our mothers, fathers, grandmothers and grandfathers, in the histories, and the stories, all the others, they all are always little babies grown old men and women or as children for us. No, old generations and past ages never have grown young men and women in them. So long ago they were, why they must be old grown men and women or as babies or as children. No, them we never can feel as young grown men and women. Such only are ourselves and our friends with whom we have been living.

And so now we begin, and with such men and women as we have old or as very little, in us, to our thinking.

One of these women, the grandmothers old always to us the generation of grandchildren, was a sweet good woman, strong just to bear many children and then she died away and left them for that was all she knew then to do for them.

Like all good older women she had all her life born many children and she had made herself a faithful working woman to her husband who was a good enough ordinary older man.

He was just a decent honest good-enough man to do ordinary working. He always was good to his wife and he always liked her to be with him, and to have good children, and to help him with her working. He always liked all of his children and he always did all that he could to help them, but they were all soon strong enough to leave him, and now that his wife had died away and left him, he was not really needed much by the world or by his children.

They were good daughters and sons to him, but his sayings and his old ordinary ways of doing had not much importance for them. They were strong, all of them, in their work and in their new way of feeling and full always of their new ways of living. It was alright, he always said it to them, and he thought it so really in him, but it was all too new, it could never be any comfort to him. He had been left out of all life while he was still living. It was all too new for his feeling and his wife was no longer there to stay beside him. He felt it always in him and he sighed and at last he just slowly left off living.

Henry Dehning was a grown man and for his day a rich one when his father died away and left them. Truly he had made everything for himself very different; but it is not as a young man making himself rich that we are now to feel him, he is for us an old grown man telling it all over to his children.

He is a middle aged man now when he talks about it all to his children, middle aged as perhaps sometimes we ourselves are now to our talking, but he, he is grown old man to our thinking. Yes truly this Henry Dehning had made everything for himself to be very different. His ways and his needs and how much money it took now to live to be decent, and all the habits of his daily life, they were all now for him very different.

And it is strange how all forget when they have once made things for themselves to be very different. A man like Dehning never can feel it real to himself, things as they were in his early manhood, now that he has made his life and habits and his feelings all so different. He says it often, as we all do childhood and old age and pain and sleeping, but it can never anymore be really present to his feeling.

Yes, they say it long and often and yet it is never real to them while they are thus talking. No it is not as really present to their thinking as it is to the young ones who never really had the feeling. These have it through their fear, which makes it for them a really present feeling. The old ones have not such a fear and they have it all only like a dim beginning, like the being as babies or as children or as grown old men and women.

And this father Dehning was always very full of such talking. He had made everything for himself and for his children. He was a good and honest man was Henry Dehning. He was strong and rich and good tempered and respected and he showed it in his look, that look that makes young people think older ones are very aged, and he loved to tell it over to his children, how he had made it all for them so they could have it and not have to work to make it different.

"Yes, what, well, tell me, you all like to be always explaining to me, tell me exactly what you are going to get from all these your expensive modern ways of doing. You know I like to get good value for my money, I always had a name for being pretty good at trading, I say, you know I like to know just what I am getting for my money and you children do certainly cost a great deal of my money, now I say, tell me, I am glad to listen to you, I say you tell me just what you are going to do, to make it good all this money."

The children laughed, "You see you can't tell yet sir," they answered, "it will be different but I guess we will be good for something."

The young Dehnings had all been born and brought up in the town of Bridgepoint. Their mother too had been born in Bridgepoint. It was there that they had first landed, her father, a harsh man, hard to his wife and to her children but not very good with all his fierceness at knowing how to make a living, and her mother a good gentle wife who never left him, though surely he was not worthy to have her so faithful to him, and she was a good woman who with all her woe was strong to bear many children and always after she was strong to do her best for them and always strong to suffer with them.

And this harsh hard man and this good gentle wife had many children, and one daughter had long ago married Henry Dehning. It was a happy marriage enough for both of them, their faults and the good things they each had in them made of them a man and wife to very well content all who had to do with them.

All the Dehnings were very fond of Bridgepoint. They had their city and their country house like all the people who were well to do in Bridgepoint.

The Dehnings in the country were simple pleasant people. It was surprising how completely they could shed there the straining luxury and uneasy importance of their city life. Their country house was one of those large commodious wooden double affairs with a wide porch all around and standing well back from the road. In front and at the sides were pleasant lawns and trees and beyond were green open marshes leading down to salt water. In back was a cleared space that spread out into great meadows of stunted oaks no higher than a man's waist, great levels glistening green in the summer and brilliantly red in the autumn stretching away under vast skies, and always here and there was a great tree waving in the wind and wading knee deep in the rough radiant leafy tide.

Yes the Dehnings in the country were simple pleasant people. All day the young ones played and bathed and rode and then the family altogether would sail and fish. The Dehning country house was very pleasant too for all young men and boys, the uncles and the cousins of the Dehning family, who all delighted in the friendly freedom of this country house, rare in those days among this kind of people, and so the Dehning house was always full of youth and kindly ways and sport and all altogether there they all always lead a pleasant family life.

The Dehning family itself was made up of the parents and three children. They made a group very satisfying to the eye, prosperous and handsome.

Mr. Dehning was a man successful, strong-featured, gentle tempered, joyous and carrying always his fifty years of life with the good-nature of a cheerful boy. He enjoyed the success that he could boast that he had won, he loved the struggle in which he had always been and always conquered, he was proud of his past and of his present worth, he was proud in his three children and proud that they could teach him things he did not know, he was proud of his wife who was proud of such very different things. "Oh Miss Jenny, she is the best girl I know," he always sang as he came to find her, never content long out of sight of his family when not engrossed by business or cards.

I said that Henry Dehning's wife was proud of such very different things, but that was wrong, she was proud

9

in a very different fashion but proud of the same things. And like him too she was very proud of her three educated children but to her thinking there was very little they could teach her. But she was very proud of these educated children and she was very proud of her husband Henry Dehning though she knew he always did little things so badly and that he would still always play like a poor man with his fingers and that he never would learn not to do it. Yes she was very proud of her husband though he always did little things so badly and she had always to be telling him how a man in his position should know how to do it. She came towards him now when he was through with his talking, and she had one rebuke to him for his always calling her his girl Miss Jenny, and another for the way he had of fidgeting always with his fingers. "Don't do that Henry!" she said to him loudly.

Mrs. Dehning was the quintessence of loud-voiced good-looking prosperity. Yes Mrs. Dehning was a woman whose rasping insensibility to gentle courtesy deserved the prejudice one cherished against her, but she was a woman, to do her justice, generous and honest, one whom one might like better the more one saw her less.

The Dehning family was made of this father and mother and three children. Mr. Dehning was very proud of his children and proud of all the things he knew that they could teach him. There were two daughters and a son of them.

Julia Dehning was named after her grandmother, but, as her father often told her, she never looked the least bit like her and yet there was a little in her that made the old world not all lost to her, a little that made one always remember that her grandmother and her father had always a worn old world to remember.

Julia Dehning was now just eighteen and she showed in all its vigor the self-satisfied crude domineering American girlhood that was strong inside her. Perhaps she was born too near the old world to ever attain quite altogether that crude virginity that makes the American girl safe in all her liberty. Yes the American girl is a crude virgin and she is safe in her freedom.

And now, so thought her mother, and Julia was quite of the same opinion, the time had come for Julia to have a husband and to begin her real important living.

Under Julia's very American face, body, clothes and manner and her vigor of the domineering and crude virgin, there were now and then flashes of passion that lit up an older well hidden tradition. Julia was much given to hearty joyous laughing and to an ardent honest feeling, and she hit the ground as she walked with the same hard jerking with which her mother Mrs. Dehning always rebuked her husband's sinning. Yes Julia Dehning was bright and full of vigor, and with something always a little harsh in her, making underneath her young bright vigorous ardent honest feeling a little of the sense of rasping that was just now in her mother's talking.

And so those who read much in story books surely now can tell what to expect of her, and yet, please reader, remember that this is perhaps not the whole of our story either, neither her father for her, nor the living down the mother who is in her, for I am not ready yet to take away the character from our Julia, for truly she may work out as the story books would have her or we may find all different kinds of things for her, and so reader, please remember, the future is not yet certain for her, and be you well warned reader, from the vain-glory of being sudden in your judgement of her.

After Julia came the boy George and he was not named after his grandfather. And so it was right that in his name he should not sound as if he were the son of his father, so at least his mother decided for him, and the father, he laughed and let her do the way she liked it. And so the boy was named George and the other was there but hidden as an initial to be only used for signing.

The boy George bade fair to do credit to his christening. George Dehning now about fourteen was strong in sport and washing. He was not foreign in his washing. Oh, no, he was really an American.

It's a great question this question of washing. One never can find anyone who can be satisfied with anybody else's washing. I knew a man once who never as far as any one could see ever did any washing, and yet he described another with contempt, why he is a dirty hog sir, he never does any washing. The French tell me it's the Italians who never do any washing, the French and the Italians both find the Spanish a little short in their washing, the English find all the world lax in this business of washing, and the East finds all the West a pig, which never is clean with just the little cold water washing.

Even the man who, when he wants to take a little hut in the country to live in, and they said to him, but there is no water to have there, and he said, what does that matter, in this country one can always have wine for his drinking, he too has others who for him don't think enough about their washing; and then there is the man who takes the bath-tub out of his house because he don't believe in promiscuous bathing; and then there is the virtuous poor woman who brings her child to the dispensary for a treatment and the doctor says to her, no I won't touch her now anymore until you clean her, and the woman cries out in her indignation, what you think I am poor like a beggar, I got money enough to pay for a doctor, I show you I can hire a real doctor, and she slams the door and rushes out with her daughter. All this washing business is certainly most peculiar.

And then when we are all through with the pleasant summer and its gorgeous washing, then comes the dreadful question of the winter washing. It's easy enough to wash often when the sun is hot and they are sticky and perspiring and the water in a natural kind of way is always flowing, but when it comes to be nasty cold as it always is in winter, then it is not any more a pleasure, it is a harsh duty then and hard to follow.

Yes, George Dehning was not at all foreign in his washing, but for him, too, the old world was not altogether lost behind him. Sometimes the boy had a way with him, and it would now show clear in spite of the fair cheery sporty nature he had in him, a way of looking sleepy and reflecting, and his lids would never be really ever very open, and he would be always only half showing his clear grey eyes that, very often, were bright alive and laughing.

And then there was the littlest one whose name had been all given without regard to the old world behind them. They called her Hortense for that was both elegant and new then. The father let the mother do as she liked with the naming, he laughed and a little he did not like it in him and then a little he was proud of his Miss Jenny and her way of doing.

The little Hortense was not of much importance yet in the family living. Hortense was ten now and full of adoration for her big sister and yet most of all for her brother. George was always very moral and too he was very hopeful. He always began his tomorrow with himself full of firm resolution to do all things every minute and to do them all very complicatedly. George felt always he must bring up this little sister for he George was the only one who knew the right ways for her. And so he preached a great deal to her, and the little Hortense was very devout and adored her instructor. There was always a dependent loyal up-gazing sweetness in her.

She was not just then very much with her mother for she was not at this time very important to her. The mother was so busy with her Julia, to find an important and good husband for her. For us now as well as for the mother the important matter in the history of the Dehning family is the marrying of Julia.

Julia as a little girl had had the usual experiences of governess guarded children. She was first the confidant, then the advisor, and last the arranger of the love affairs of her established guardians. She learnt very well all the things young girls of her class were taught then and she learnt too, in all kinds of ways, all the things girls always can learn, somehow, to be wise in. And so Julia was well prepared now to be a woman. She had singing and piano-playing and sport and all regular school learning, she had good looks, honesty, and brilliant courage, and in her young way a certain kind of wisdom.

There is nothing more joyous than being healthful young and energetic, and loving movement sunshine and clean air. Combine all this with owning of a horse and courage enough to ride him wildly, and God is good to overflowing to his children. It is pleasant too to have occasionally a sympathetic comrade on such rides. Jameson was a pleasant man of thirty five or thereabouts, a good free rider and an easy talker. Julia knew him first at home and met him usually while riding to the station to meet her father and the city train. It was all very pleasant and unaggressive, but Julia began to notice that Mrs. Jameson frowned on her in anger now, whenever they all met together. Then too Jameson grew gradually less comradely, more intimate, and gross. Julia understood at last and did not ride with him again.

Such incidents as these are common in the lives of all young women and are only important in those intenser natures that, by their understanding, make each incident into a situation. Such natures suck a full experience from every act, and live so much in what, to others, means so little, for is it not common and to be expected.

In Julia Dehning all experience had gone to make her wise now in a desire for a master in the art of life, and it came to pass that in Alfred Hersland brought by a cousin to visit at the house she found a man who embodied her ideal in a way to make her heart beat with surprise. To a bourgeois mind that has within it a little of the fervor for diversity, there can be nothing more attractive than a strain of singularity that yet keeps well within the limits of conventional respectability, a singularity that is, so to speak, well dressed and well set up.

Now singularity that is neither crazy, sporty, faddish, or a fashion, or low class with distinction, such a singularity, I say, we have not made enough of yet so that any other one can really know it, it is as yet an unknown product with us. It takes time to make queer people, and to have others who can know it, time and a certainty of place and means. Custom, passion, and a feel for mother earth are needed to breed vital singularity in any man, and alas, how poor we are in all these three.

Brother Singulars, we are misplaced in a generation that knows not Joseph. We flee before the disapproval of our cousins, the courageous condescension of our friends who gallantly sometimes agree to walk the streets with us, from all them who never any way can understand why such ways and not the others are so dear to us, we fly to the kindly comfort of an older world accustomed to take all manner of strange forms into its bosom and we leave our noble order to be known under such forms as Alfred Hersland, a poor thing, and even hardly then our own.

The Herslands were a Western family. David Hersland, the father, had gone out to a Western state to make his money. His wife had been born and brought up in the town of Bridgepoint. Later Mr. Hersland had sent his son Alfred back there to go to college and then to stay on and to study to become a lawyer. Now it was some years later and Alfred Hersland had come again to Bridgepoint, to settle down there to practice law there, and to make for himself his own money.

The Hersland family had not had their money any longer than the others of this community, but they had taken to culture and to ideas quicker.

Hersland was tall and well dressed and sufficiently good-looking, and he carried himself always with a certain easy dignity and grace. His blond hair, which he wore parted in the middle, a way of doing which at that time showed both courage and conviction, covered a well shaped head. His eyes and voice meant knowledge, feeling and a certain mystery.

Julia Dehning threw herself eagerly into this new acquaintance. She no longer wanted that men should bring with them the feel of out of doors, for out of doors with men now was soiled to her sense by the grossness of the Jamesons. Alfred Hersland brought with him the world of art and things, a world to her but vaguely known.

Not many months from this first meeting, Julia gave her answer. "Yes, I do care for you," she said, "and you and I will live our lives together, always learning things and doing things, good things they will be for us whatever other people may think or say."

She had had, always, stirring within her, a longing for the knowledge of made things, of works of art, of all the wonders that make, she knew, a world, for certain other people. It was a very real desire, this longing for the wisdom of all culture, this that had been always strong in Julia. Of course, mostly, such longing in Julia, took the form of moral idealism, the only form of culture the spare American imagination takes natural refuge in.

Of the family about her, it was only Julia who found him worthy to be so important to her. The cousins and the uncles, the men who could make for her the sane and moral background that would give a wholesome middle class condition always to her, they did not like it much that Hersland was now so important to her. They said nothing to her, but they did not like to have him always about with her. He was not their kind and every minute they could know it, and they did not need him, either out in the world in business or at home where they were happy in the rich and solid family comfort they always had had with the Dehnings; and these men could not find Hersland's knowledge worth much for them, and they did not have it in them that it had a meaning for them that he Hersland had in him, knowledge and a certain kind of feeling that they never could have inside them. What could a pleasant mystery in a man mean to them except only that any man with any sense in him would not ever trust anything real to him.

The boy George and the little sister were too young to think very much about him. The young brother did not feel it in himself much to like him, for young George you may remember was young and heroic, out of doors was not yet in any way soiled for him and he needed that kind of man to attract him, but anyhow, Julia liked him and it would be hard for George not to think Julia could judge better about him than any of the other members of the family could have it to know in them.

Mr. Dehning as yet had said nothing. One day he was out walking and his daughter was with him. "Julia hadn't you better be a little careful how much you encourage that young Hersland."

Mr. Dehning, always, in his working, began very far away from a thing he meant later to be firmly attacking.

"Why papa!" she had eagerly quickly demanded of him.

"I say Julia I don't know anything against him. I have looked up all the record there is yet of him and I haven't heard anything against him but Julia, I say, somehow I don't quite like him." "Isn't that papa because he plays the piano and parts his hair that way in the middle." Julia was eager in her questioning. The father laughed, "I guess there is some reason in your question Julia, I don't like that kind of thing much in a man, that's right. Anyhow Julia I think you better be a little careful with him."

Henry Dehning had had a long time to learn how to judge the value in a man, the values in them that in their lives concerned him.

"You know Julia" Mr. Dehning went on after a silent interval of walking when they had each been pretty busy with their own thinking, "you know Julia, your mother doesn't like him." "Oh! mamma!" Julia broke out, "you know how mamma is, he talks about love and beauty and mamma thinks it ought to be all wedding dresses and a fine house when it isn't money and business. She would be the same about anybody that I would want."

So Julia struggled every day, to have him, arguing discoursing explaining and appealing. She was always winning but it was slow progress like that in very steep and slippery climbing. For every forward movement of three feet she always slipped back two, sometimes all three and often four and five and six and seven. It was long eager steady fighting but the father was slowly understanding that his daughter wanted this thing enough to stand hard by it and with such feeling and no real fact against the man, such a father was bound to let her some time get married to him.

"I tell you what Julia what I have been thinking. When we all get back to town you can tell better whether you do really want him. I don't say no Julia and I don't say yes to you. When everybody gets back to town and you are busy and running around with your girls and talking and meeting all the other people and the other kinds of young men, you can tell much better then whether all this business is not all just talking with you. I say Julia I don't say no to you and I don't say yes yet to you."

And so at last, filled full with faith and hope and a fine new joy she went back to her busy city life, strong in the passion of her eager young imagining.

The home the rich and self made merchant makes to hold his family and himself is always like the city where his fortune has been made. In London it is like that rich and endless dark and gloomy place, in Paris it is filled with pleasant toys, cheery and light and made of gilded decoration and white paint, and in Bridgepoint it was neither gloomy nor yet joyous but like a large and splendid canvas completely painted over but painted full of empty space.

It was good solid riches in the Dehning house, a parlor full of ornate marbles placed on yellow onyx stands, chairs gold and white of various size and shape, a delicate blue silk brocaded covering on the walls and a ceiling painted pink with angels and cupids all about, a dining room all dark and gold, a living room all rich and gold and red with built-in-couches, glass-covered book-cases and paintings of well washed peasants of the german school, and large and dressed up bedrooms all light and blue and white. Marble and bronzes and crystal chandeliers and gas logs finished out each room. And always everywhere there were complicated ways to wash, and dressing tables full with brushes, sponges, instruments, and ways to make one clean, and to help out all the special doctors in their work.

It was good solid riches in this house and here it was that Julia Dehning dreamed of other worlds and here each day she grew more firm in her resolve for that wide free and cultured life to which for her young Hersland had the key.

And so the marriage was really to be made. Mrs. Dehning now all reconciled and eager, began the trousseau and the preparation of the house that the young couple were to have as a wedding portion from the elder Dehnings.

In dresses, hats and shoes and gloves and underwear, and jewel ornaments, Julia was very ready to follow her mother in her choice and to agree with her in all variety and richness of trimming in material, but in the furnishing of her own house it must be as she wished, taught as she now had been that there were things of beauty in the world and that decoration should be strange and like old fashions, not be in the new. To have the older things themselves had not yet come to her to know, nor just how old was the best time that they should be.

In ways to wash, to help out all the special doctors in their work, in sponges, brushes, running water everywhere, in hygienic ways to air things and to keep ones self and everything all clean, this house that Julia was to make fit for her new life which was to come, in this it was very like the old one she had lived in, but always there were more plunges, douches, showers, ways to get cold water, luxury in freezing, in hardening, than her mother's house had ever afforded to them. In her mother's house there were many ways to get clean but they mostly suggested warm water and a certain comfort, here in the new house was a sterner feeling, it must be a cold world, that one could keep one's soul high and clean in.

All through this new house there were no solid warm substantial riches. There were no silks in curtains, no blue brocade here, no glass chandeliers to make prisms and give tinklings. Here the parlor was covered with modern solemn tapestry, the ceiling all in tone the chairs as near to good colonial as modern imitation can effect, and all about dark aesthetic ornaments from China and Japan. Paintings there were none, only carbon photographs framed close, in dull and wooden frames.

The dining room was without brilliancy, for there can be no brilliancy in a real aesthetic aspiration. The chairs were made after some old french fashion, not very certain what, and covered with dull tapestry, copied without life from old designs, the room was all a discreet green with simple oaken wood-work underneath. The living rooms were a prevailing red, that certain shade of red like that certain shade of green, dull, without hope, the shade that so completely bodies forth the ethically aesthetic aspiration of the spare American emotion. Everywhere were carbon photographs upon the walls sadly framed in painted wooden frames. Free couches, open book-cases, and fire places with really burning logs, finished out each room.

These were triumphant days for Julia. Every day she led her family a new flight and they followed after agape with wonder disapproval and with pride.

But always, a little, through all this pride in domination and in the admiration of her family, there was there, somewhere, in the background, to her sense, a vague uncertain kind of feeling as to her understanding and her right. Mostly she had a firm strong feeling in her, but always, a little, there was there, a kind of doubting somewhere in her. Hersland was safe, though very simply now, he often made for her that sharp uncertain feeling more dreadful and more clear before her. He was not different in his ways or in his talk to her from the way he had always been with her, but somehow now it had come to her, to see, as dying men are said to see, clearly and freely things as they are and not as she had wished them to be for her.

And then she would remember suddenly what she had really thought he was, and she felt, she knew that all that former thought was truer better judgement than this sudden sight, and so she dulled her momentary clearing mind and hugged her old illusions to her breast.

In a few days more the actual marrying was done and their lives together always doing things and learning things was at last begun.

Bear it in your mind my reader, but truly I never feel it that there ever can be for me any such a creature, no it is this scribbled and dirty and lined paper that is really to be to me always my receiver — but anyhow reader, bear it in your mind — that this that I write down a little each day here on my scraps of paper for you is not just an ordinary kind of novel with a plot and conversations to amuse you, but a record of a decent family progress respectably lived by us and our fathers and our mothers, and our grand-fathers and grand-mothers, and this is by me carefully a little each day to be written down here; and so my readers arm yourself in every kind of way to be patient, and to be eager, for you must always have it now before you to hear much more of these many kinds of decent ordinary people, of old, grown, grand-fathers and grand-mothers, of growing old fathers and growing old mothers, of ourselves who are always to be young grown men and women for us, and then there are still to be others and we must wait and see the younger fathers and young mothers bear them for us, these younger fathers and young mothers who are always ourselves inside us, who are to be always young grown men and women to us. And so listen while I tell you all about us, and wait while I hasten slowly forwards, and love, please, this history of this decent family's progress.

The Herslands were a western family. David Hersland as a young man had gone far into the new country to make his money. He had settled down in Gossols and had lived there for twenty years and more now.

He had made a big fortune. David Hersland was in some ways a splendid kind of person.

The Herslands had never had a city house to be restless around them and to give restlessness inside to them. They had all these years been in the place they now lived in. This house they had always lived in was not in the part of Gossols where the other rich people mostly were living. It was an old place left over from the days when Gossols was just beginning. It was grounds about ten acres large, fenced in with just ordinary kind of rail fencing, it had a not very large wooden house standing on the rising ground in the center with a winding avenue of eucalyptus, blue gum, leading from it to the gateway. It was very wonderful there in the summer with the dry heat, and the sun burning, and the hot earth for sleeping and then in the winter with the rain, and the north wind blowing that would bend the trees and often break them, and the owls in the walls scaring you with their tumbling.

All the rest of the ten acres was for hay and a little vegetable gardening and an orchard with all the kinds of fruit trees that could be got there to do any growing.

In the summer it was good for generous sweating to help the men make hay into bails for its preserving and it was well for ones growing to eat radishes pulled with the black earth sticking to them and to chew the mustard and find roots with all kinds of funny flavors in them, and to fill ones hat with fruit and sit on the dry ploughed ground and eat and think and sleep and read and dream and never hear them when they would all be calling; and then when the quail came it was fun to go shooting, and then when the wind and the rain and the ground were ready to help seeds in their growing, it was good fun to help plant them, and the wind would be so strong it would blow the leaves and branches of the trees down around them and you could shout and work and get wet and be all soaking and run out full into the strong wind and let it dry you, in between the gusts of rain that left you soaking. It was fun all the things that happened all the year there then.

And all around the whole fence that shut these joys in was a hedge of roses, not wild, they had been planted, but now they were very sweet and small and abundant and all the people from that part of Gossols came to pick the leaves to make sweet scented jars and pillows, and always all the Herslands were indignant and they would let loose the dogs to bark and scare them but still the roses grew and always all the people came and took them. And altogether the Herslands always loved it there in their old home in Gossols.

David Hersland's mother was a good foreign woman who was strong to bear many children and always after was very strong to lead them. The old woman was a great mountain. She had it in her to uphold around her, her man, her family, and everybody else whom she saw needing directing. She had a few weak ways in her toward some of them, mostly toward one of them who had a bad way of eating too much and being weak and loving, and his mother never could be strong to correct him, no she could not be strong to let his brothers try and save him, and so he died a glutton, but the old mother was dead too by then and she did not have the sorrow of seeing what came to him.

She led her family out of the old world into the new one and there they learned through her and by themselves, almost every one of them, how to make for themselves each one a sufficient fortune. Yes it was she who led them all out of the old world into the new one. The father was not a man to do any such leading. He was a butcher by trade. He was a very gentle creature in his nature. He loved to sit and think and he loved to be important in religion. He was a small man, well enough made, with a nice face, blue eyes, and a little lightish colored beard. He loved his eating and a quiet life, he loved his Martha and his children, and mostly he liked all the world.

It would never come to him to think of a new world. He would go, — yes to be sure it would be very nice there, only it was very nice here and here he was important in religion, — and he liked his village and his shop and everything he had known all his life there, and the house they had had ever since he married his good Martha and settled himself to be comfortable with her, — and now they had their children. Yes, alright, perhaps, maybe she was right, there was no reason, the neighbors had all gotten so rich going to America, there was no reason they shouldn't go and get rich there, alright he would go if his Martha talked about it so much to him, alright, his Martha could fix it any way she liked it, yes it would be nice to have all of them get rich there. Yes the neighbors always were sending money to their father when he needed to have it. Alright they would all go, his Martha could fix it any way she liked it.

Martha began then and she soon sold their business and the things on the little farm and in the shop and in their house, and kept only the few things she knew they needed. Her man liked it very well then this being so important and he could use it as he liked to do religion. He liked it very well to see his wife do all this selling. He liked the feeling he had in him when they were all so busy buying and selling all around him, but when the people came to take the things he had been so important about when his wife was selling, then it was a very different feeling he had in him.

It had been very pleasant to him. He never really had to do any deciding, and he had all the emotion and the important feeling, it was just like in religion.

But it was not so pleasant for him when the people came and took the things it had been so pleasant selling. It hurt him to have the things he loved go away from him, and he wanted to give back the money to all of them so that he could keep them. But he knew that that could not be done and he still keep his important feeling that was so pleasant to him; and then too Martha would not let him. He said nothing to the people when they came to take the things it had been so pleasant selling to them, he was only very slow in giving the things to them. He would lose them so that it was very hard to find them but the children and Martha always found them.

But now it was all done and they were all of them ready to do the last beginning. All the things they had kept had been put on the wagon, the littlest children were to ride on top of them, the rest were to walk beside them until they came to the city by the water where they would find the ship that was to take them to that new world where they were all to make a fortune.

They started very well the next morning, with all the people to say good-bye to them and with all the things they needed piled in the wagon, the littlest children set on top of them, the rest of them to walk beside them. The mother was like a great mountain, good and firm and directing, and as always able to uphold around her, her man, her children, and everybody who needed directing, and he was feeling it once more good inside him to be important as if it were in religion, and all the talking and moving and everybody so excited about him. It was very pleasant just then for him, and then the wagon began moving, and some went a little way with them and then they all left them and then it was only the family and the driver of the wagon who were with him and all the pleasant feeling left him.

They went on and on and then suddenly they missed him, the father was not there any longer with them. The mother went back patiently to find him. He was sitting at the first turning, looking at the village below him, at all the things he was leaving, and he simply could not endure it in him.

His wife called to him. He sighed and she came to him. "If you don't really want to be going you've just got to say David what you want to be doing. You just say David what it is you are really wanting. The children, they are all waiting there just for you to say it. David I say you just say it what you want and I do it." He sighed and he looked a little sullen.

"It's just I wanted to see what way it looked so I could get it right not to forget it. I just look to see I got it fixed right so I don't forget it." And he sighed and he got up and he looked back as he went away from it and she talked about how much the children were going to like it and he began to forget it.

All, the wagon and the driver and the horses and the children, had waited for them to come up to it. Now they went on again, slowly and creaking, as is the way always when a whole family do it. Moving through a country is never done very quickly when a whole family do it.

They were all having now just coming in them their first tired, the first hot sense of being very tired. This is the hardest time in a day's walking to press through and get over being tired until it comes to the last tired, that last dead tired sense that is so tired. Then you cannot press through to a new strength and to get another tired, you just keep on, that is you keep on when you have learned how you can do it, then you just get hardened to it and know there is no pressing through it, there is no way to win out beyond it, it is just a dreary dull dead tired, and you must learn to know it, and it is always and you must learn to bear it, the dull drag of being almost dead with being tired.

In between these first and last there are many little times of tired, many ways of being very tired, but never any like the first hot tired when you begin to learn how to press through it and never any like the last dead tired with no beyond ever to it.

It was this first hot tired they all had in them now just in its beginning, and they were all in their various ways trying to press themselves to go through it, and they were mostly very good about it and not impatient or complaining. They were all now beginning with the dull tired sense of hot trudging when every step has its conscious meaning and all the movement is as if one were lifting each muscle and every part of the skin as a separate action. It is not until one has settled to it, the steady walk where one is not conscious of the movement, that you have become really strong to do it, and the whole family were now just coming to it, they were just pressing through their first hot tired.

And now once more the father had done it. The father was no longer with them, once more he had slipped back and they had lost him.

The mother said to the children. "Well you go on, I go back to find him." She felt no anger toward him. She just went patiently back to find him. She walked back looking patiently everywhere for him. She found him before she had gotten back to where she had the last time found him. She had walked faster than he and had caught him.

She had no impatient feeling in her against him. It was a way he had, she knew it, it was right for him to have it, the kind of feeling he had about leaving. It was right for him to act that way to see about not forgetting. It was just his way and now she would coax him and he would come back with her to the wagon. Soon they came up with the wagon which was still very slowly moving.

It was so hot doing so much walking, she said then to him, he looked a little sick, she thought he ought not to do any more walking, perhaps it would be better if he would get into the wagon and ride a little with the little children. It would be awful if he got sick and nobody to take care of them for he was the only one that could do their talking. And so she coaxed him into the wagon with the children.

They went on and soon it was too far, there was not now anymore going back for him. And then he was content, and he had the new city and the ship, and then he was content with the new world around him.

They had, for a little while, a hard time beginning, but on the whole things went very well with them. The sons made money for them, the daughters worked and then got married to men whom they found making money around them. Some did very well then and some not so well, and they all had their troubles as all people have them, and some died, and some lived and were prosperous and had children. One as I was saying died a glutton and spoiling him was the one weak thing the strong mother did to harm any of them.

The old man never made much of a fortune but with the help his children gave him he lived very well and when he died he left his wife a nice little fortune. She lived long and was strong to the last and firmly supporting and her back was straight and firm and always she was like a great mountain, and always she was directing and leading all whom she found needing directing.

She was then very old, and always well, and always working, and then she had a stroke, and then another, and then she died and that was the end of that generation.

There had been born to Martha and David Hersland many sons and daughters. One, the glutton, died and left his wife and children to his brothers, he had not made enough money to leave them provided, and his brothers each one in their turn gave the money to support them. Of the daughters two of them were well married. The third of them always lived with her husband but it was her brothers who kept her dressed and gave her children education and then later in their life started them out in their working.

The fourth son, David Hersland, one of the fathers we must soon be realizing so that we can understand our own being, was the only one of all of them who had gone to the far west to make his fortune. He was big and abundant and full of new ways of thinking, and this was all his mother in him, but he had not her patient steadfast working. He was irritable and impatient and uncertain and not always very strong at keeping going, though always he was abundant and forceful and joyous and determined and always powerful in starting. And then too he was in his way important inside to him as his father had been when he felt his religion in him. But all this will show more and more in him as I tell you slowly the history of him.

As I was saying he had brought his wife to Gossols with him. Fanny Hersland all her life was a sweet gentle little woman. Not that she did not have a fierce little temper sometimes in her and one that could be very stubborn, but mostly she was a sweet little gentle mother woman and only would be hurt, not angry, when any bad thing happened to them.

Her mother was one of those good foreign women the grandmothers, always old women or as little children to us the generation of grandchildren. These good foreign women, the grandmothers we need only to be just remembering, had each one a different kind of foreign man to be a master to them.

The gentle little hopeless one who wept out all the sorrow for her children had many and very little children. The little weary weeping mother of all these gentle cheery little children had a foreign husband who was not very pleasant to his children. He too was little like his wife and like all his children but there was a great deal in him to cause terror to his wife and children. He was like old David Hersland important in religion. It was very deep inside him and with him it was much harder on his children. His wife too had sorrow in religion, she had sorrow from his being so important in religion and she had sorrow too from her own self in her own religion.

But then it was all sorrow and sadness, and always a trickling kind of weeping that she had every moment in her living, and it was really not much worse in religion.

It was a hard father and a dreary mother that gave the world so many and such pleasant little children. Perhaps it was that the mother had wept out all the sorrow for them. There was no weeping that she had left over to them. They were mostly all in their later living cheerful hopeful gentle little men and women. They lived without ambition or excitement but they were each in their little circle joyful in the present. They lived and died in mildness and contentment.

It was one of these gentle little Hissen people that David Hersland married there in Bridgepoint and then took to Gossols with him. They had had five children through her. Two of these had died as little children. Three of them had grown up and were now grown young men and women, and these three are of them who are to be always in this history of us young grown men and women to us, for it is only thus that we can ever feel them to be real inside us, them who are the same generation with us.

Now I will tell you more of the Hersland ways of living in the old home with the wind and the sun and the rain beating, and the dogs and the chickens and the open life, and the hay, and the men working, and the father's way of educating the three children so that they could be strong to make for themselves their own beginning, and the gentle little mother who was not very important to them, and the three children with the mixed up father and the little unimportant mother in them.

As I was saying Mr. Hersland was big and abundant and always very full of new ways of thinking. Always he was abundant and joyous and determined and always powerful in starting. Also sometimes he would be irritable and impatient and uncertain. Also he was in his way important inside to him, and all these things came out in his educating of his children. One never knew which way it would break out from him the things he was very good at starting and then other things would happen to him and to all the people around who were dependent on him.

It was a very good kind of living the Hersland children had in their beginning, and their freedom in the ten acres where all kinds of things were growing, where they could have all anybody could want of joyous sweating, of rain and wind, of hunting, of cows and dogs and horses, of chopping wood, of making hay, of dreaming, of lying in a hollow all warm with the sun shining while the wind was howling, of knowing all queer poor kinds of people that lived in this part of Gossols where the Herslands were living and where no other rich people were living.

Altogether it was a good way of living for them who had a passion to be free inside them and this was true of all three of the Hersland children but mostly with Martha the eldest and the only daughter living, and the youngest David who was always searching to decide in him and no one could ever understand him, from day to day what life meant to him to make it worth his living. It was less in Alfred, this love of freedom, in Alfred who was soon now to be marrying Julia Dehning. He had some of it in him but not so strongly inside him as Martha and David and his father had it in them.

Yes real singularity we have not made enough of yet so that any other one can really know it. I say vital singularity is as yet an unknown product with us, we who in our habits, dress-suit cases, clothes and hats and ways of thinking, walking, making money, talking, having simple lines in decorating, in ways of reforming, all with a metallic clicking like the type-writing which is our only way of thinking, our way of educating, our way of learning, all always the same way of doing, all the way down as far as there is any way down inside to us. We are all the same all through us, we never have it to be free inside us.

It is hard on children when the father has queer ways in him. Even when they love him they can never keep themselves from having shame inside them when all the people are looking and wondering and laughing and giving him a name for the queer ways of him.

David Hersland was a big man. His eyes were brown and sharp and piercing and sometimes dancing with laughing and often angry with irritation. His hands would be quiet a long time and then impatient in their moving. He never would go so far as his irritation seemed to drive him, and somehow one always knew that of him. He had not so much terror for his children as fathers with more kindness and more steadfast ways of doing. And so each one of the three children, Martha, Alfred and David would each in their own way resist him, and it made a household where there was much fierce talking

38

and much frowning, and then the father would end with pounding on the table and threatening and saying that he was the father and they were the children, he was the master, they must obey else he would know the way to make them. And the little unimportant mother would be all lost then in between the angry father and the three big resentful children. But all this was when they were beginning to be grown young men and women. When they were still children there was not any fierceness in the house among them.

As I was saying the father was a big man. He liked eating, he liked strange ways of educating his children and he was always changing, and sometimes he was very generous to them and then he would change toward them and it would be hard for them to get even little things that they needed in the position that was given to them by their father's fortune and large way of living.

In the street in his walking, and it was then his children were a little ashamed of him, he always had his hat back on his head so that it always looked as if it were falling, and he would march on, he was a big man and loved walking, with two or three of his children following behind him or with one beside him, and he was always forgetting all about them, and everybody would stop short to look at him, accustomed as they were to see him, for he had a way of tossing his head to get freedom and a way of muttering to himself in his thinking and he had always a movement of throwing his body and his shoulders from side to side as he was arguing to himself about things he wanted to be changing, and always he had the important feeling to himself inside him. As he would be walking along with a child beside him or several of them behind him, he would stop and sweep the prospect with his cane and begin talking and somebody near him would come to listen. It was just ordinary talking that he would be doing, about the weather or the country or the fruit and it did not seem to have any deep meaning but it was the power and completeness of the identification of this big man with all creation that forced people to think of him.

And so he would stand talking and the unhappy uncomfortable child beside him would keep saying, when he was not afraid to break in on him, "Come on papa all those people are looking." "What!" the father was not listening to him but would keep right on with his talking. The child as much as he dared would twitch or pull at him, "What!" but the father never really heard him and he would go on with the queer ways in him. Slowly his children learned endurance of him. Later in their life they were queer too like him.

Often when he was walking with his children and passed a shop and saw some fruit or cakes or something that pleased him he took it and gave it to his children and they would be most uncomfortable then and say something about not wanting it to him. "What!" and he never listened to them. The children suffered so because they were not sure that the man inside knew that their father would pay him. The child never did learn that the fruit man would not be worried with him, that they all knew his father and the queer ways of him, and that the father always paid him. The fruit men all knew him and liked the abundant world embracing feeling of him and they liked to see him, but his children never could lose, until they grew up to be queer themselves each one inside him, the uncomfortable feeling that his queer ways gave them.

To him, David Hersland, education was almost the whole of living. In it was always the making of a new beginning, the having ideas, and often changing. And then there were so many ways of considering the question.

There were so many ways of seeing the meaning of the various parts that made education. There was the health, the mind, the notion of right living, the learning cooking and all useful things that he knew they should know now to be doing, and then there was his system of hardening so that they would be ready to make each one their own beginning; and all these needs for them and the many ways to look at them led to many queer things that his children had to endure from him.

Their education was a mixture of hardening, of forcing themselves into a kind of living as if they were poor people and had no one to do things for them, with a way of being very rich, that is having everything the father ever could imagine would do any good to any one of them.

They found it a great trouble to them, this past education, when they first began to be young grown men and women. Later in their living they liked it that they had had such a mixture of being rich and poor, together, in them. They never knew any one of them nor the father who was directing it for them just where their learning was coming from or how it would touch them. Mr. Hersland had all kinds of ways of seeing education. He was fondest of all of the idea of hardening but this was difficult for him to keep steadfast in him with his great interest in every kind of new invention, in wanting that his children should always have anything that could do any good to any one of them.

There was joy in them all in their later living that it had been Gossols where they had had their youthful feeling and later when they learned to know other young grown men and women they loved the freedom that they had inside them, that their father had in his queer way won for them.

As I was saying they had ten acres where they had every kind of fruit tree that could be got there to do any growing, and they had cows and dogs and horses and hay making, and the sun in the summer dry and baking, and the wind in the autumn and in the winter the rain beating and then in the spring time the hedge of roses to fence all these joys in.

Their mother had always been accustomed to a well to do middle class living, to keep a good table for her husband and the children, to dressing herself and her children in simple expensive clothing, to have the children get as presents whatever any one of them wanted to have at that time to amuse them. She was a sweet contented little woman who lived in her husband and her children, who could only know well to do middle class living, who never knew what it was her husband and her children were working out inside them and around them. When they were little children they liked to cuddle to her when she took them out to visit the rich people who lived in the other part of Gossols. They were all bashful children, living as they did in the part of the town where no rich people were living and so being used to poor queer kind of people and only feeling really at home with them who were not people in the position that their father's fortune and large way of living would naturally make companions for them. And so the little children when they went to visit with their mother in the part of Gossols where other rich people were living, they clung to her or on the sofa where she would be sitting and talking, they climbed behind her, and then too she wore seal-skins and pleasant stuffs for children to rub against and feel as rich things to touch and have near them and so they liked to go with her, and this and the habit of being children with a mother was mostly all the feeling that they had for her until later when she was ailing and the little stubborn temper in her broke into weakness and helplessness inside her and they had in a way to be good to her.

They always in a way were good to her that is as much as they could remember to think about her, but it was not important inside to any of them to remember about her neither when as children they were near her or when later she was ailing and needed them to be good to her.

This sweet gentle little mother woman who had some-times a fierce little temper in her that could be very stubborn when it arose strongly inside her, never knew really in her that she was not important to the children who had come into the world through her. She did not feel it to be important to her what other people felt for her. She knew the value of herself, and their well to do way of living, of her husband, and her nice children, and the simple expensive clothing they wore when they went out visiting to that part of Gossols where the other rich people were living. That was there. To have it gave her no important feeling. Her husband David Hersland with the queer nature of him might have an important feeling coming to him from just breathing, that feeling could come to him from the singular nature of him, from his being as big as all the world in his beginning, but to an ordinary gentle little mother woman there could never come such a feeling.

It was queer that her children were to her like well to do living, not important to her feeling.

As I was saying David Hersland had made a decent fortune even before he had left Bridgepoint. He had made enough money to give his wife and children a good position. And so when they first came to Gossols where he was to make for himself a great fortune they could afford to live in as good a hotel as was then there existing. Here Mrs. Hersland had been at first a little lonesome.

Here she had her first important feeling. Here she met a Miss Sophie Schilling and her sister Pauline Schilling and their mother old Mrs. Schilling.

Old Mrs. Schilling and her daughter Sophie Schilling and her other daughter Pauline Schilling, first gave to her the feeling of being important to herself inside her, important, apart in her, from right being, right acting, and the dignity of decent family living with good eating being the mother of nice children the wife of a good well to do man, and all the simple and expensive clothing.

All the Hissen people had it strongly inside them, the family way of good living. They never had any of them an important feeling of themselves inside them to arise of itself from within them. The little religious father who had made them all, all his children, he could not make others not living with him feel him, the little religious father who had made all of his children feel him had such an important feeling inside him, it was his religion gave it to him, it did not arise of itself from within him. He could make all his children feel him, he could in a way make them fearful of him and the religion in him, and all the religion was of him and he was in himself all there was of religion, and so it was that he had the important feeling inside in him, but this did not make any but his children feel him, it did not arise of itself inside him and he could not make any one who did not live with him feel it in him.

The little dreary mother with her trickling kind of weeping that she had every moment in her living, even, as when it sometimes happened, she was laughing, this dreary little trickling woman had with her sadness in religion and in her trickling weeping that kept on always wetting all the sorrow there could be in living, this trickling dreary little Mrs. Hissen, who wept out all the sorrow for her children, had in her an important kind of being that was almost an important feeling, and this almost an important feeling did not come to her as in her husband from religion, it arose up inside her with her trickling weeping.

Mostly the Hissen men and women the children of the father and religion and the trickling dreary mother who hardly knew how she came to make them, in all these Hissen little men and women there was never very much of such important feeling. They all of course had in them their own individual way of thinking and of doing only they never had inside them each one for himself the real important feeling.

Some of them had often a very angry feeling, some had fierce tempers and sometimes bitter biting ways of talking, some had very stubborn ways inside them, and some had it mostly in them to be only hurt not angry when any bad thing happened to them. In some of them it was a very stubborn feeling that was the deepest thing inside them after the family way that made all them, and these were the hardest to live with and never to be forgiven when they had been hurt or angry by something some one had done to them. But mostly the Hissen men and women were gentle cheerful little men and women, mostly they lived without ambition or excitement and mostly they were each in their little circle cheerful in the present.

Until they were all grown men and women, until the women each one found a husband to control them and the men went into a business and were independent of him, until they were in this sense grown men and women, until he died the father always wanted and succeeded in shutting them all up to be always with him. This was not in him from any small feeling inside him but from the important feeling he had in him of being all there was for him of religion and it was his sense of the right way for them to be as children that made him shut them up so and keep them there close to him.

Later when the daughters were married and the sons working were independent of him and had left him, he never in any way wished to interfere with them, with their feeling, their religion, their way of thinking or their doing. It was queer unless you really could understand him, could really see how the important feeling came to be in him, it was certainly queer to just ordinary thinking to see a man who had been so rigid with his children, keeping them shut up with him, making them live every minute as he would have them, having no power with any one who did not live so with him, it was queer that when these children came to be grown men and women, that is independent and living away from him, that he never in any way wanted to keep his hold on them. He had for them then as much affection as he ever had had for them, he always went to see them and was open and friendly with them but not in any way had he ever any kind of desire in him to interfere with them or their way of living or their thinking or their doing, no not even with their feeling in religion. So strong was it in him, this tolerating spirit toward them when they were grown men and women to him, that even when later in their living they sometimes asked him to guide them he would refuse it to them, for they were then apart from him, he was all there was of religion, religion was all there was of being for him; that made him important to himself inside him.

One of them who had come to be grown up for him was the Fanny Hissen who had married David Hersland. It came one day to a very great division between her husband's way of thinking and feeling in religion and her father's ways as she had learned to have them inside her when she with all her sisters and her brothers were living shut up with him.

She wrote to him and asked him, she said her husband wanted her to go with him and it was not as she had been taught by him her father, she did not feel it wrong to do this thing but she could not do it without asking her father, who had never let his children do any such thing when they were shut up with him.

The old man replied. "My dear child. There was once a priest, a good man. Once a member of his church came to him and said I have been thinking can I do this thing, can I go to a barber's shop and get shaved on a Sunday morning, is it wrong for me to do this thing. The priest said yes, he must forbid it to him, he must not go to a barber's shop on a Sunday morning and get a man to shave him, it was wrong for him to do this thing, it would be a sin in him. Two Sundays after the man met his priest coming out of a shop shaved all fresh and clean. But how is this, the man said to him, you told me that it was forbidden, you told me, when I asked you, that I should not do this thing, that it would be for me a sin. Ah! said the priest to him, that was right, I told you I must forbid you to go Sunday morning to a shop and get some one to shave you, that it would be a sin for you to do this thing, but don't you see, I did not do any asking."

And so he went on to his dying and through his being so all himself all there was of living and of religion, he was in his old age full of toleration, and slowly in his dying it was a great death that met him. Even his dead wife with her trickling crying that had been to her almost an important feeling of herself inside her, even she had been apart from him, and his children when they were no longer shut up with him were apart from him. And so he died away and left them and his important feeling died inside him.

David Hersland married Fanny Hissen. He took her out to Gossols with him. They married soon after the first meeting and then they mixed up their two natures in them and then through them there came the three children, Martha, Alfred, and young David, and these three are of them who are to be always in this history of us young grown men and women to us.

In American teaching marrying is just loving but that is not enough for marrying. Loving is alright as a beginning but then there is marrying and that is very different. In many towns there are many in each generation, decent well to do men, who keep on in their daily living and never come to any marrying. They all do a little loving. Everybody sometime does a little loving. It takes more for marrying, sometimes it needs a sister of the man to make his marrying, sometimes the mother of the girl who is to be married to him. This is not so when they are young, the man and woman, and both are lively in the feeling of loving. It is so when the man has come to be fixed in his way of living, when he finds it pleasant to go on as he is doing.

American teaching says it is all loving but all who know many families of women, all who know comfortable well to do men with a regular way of living know that it is all mostly lying that says it is loving that is strong to make a beginning, they need a sister who has already for herself her own man and children or a girl who is strong to make for herself her own winning or the mother of the girl who is to be married to him. It takes one and sometimes even all three of them and with it a fair amount of loving to make the marrying of well to do men and women.

David Hersland's sister Martha arranged his marriage for him. Martha was one of the two Hersland women who had done very well in marrying. She was a small good enough looking woman with blue eyes and with a manner that was not very unpleasant. She loved to be important by the doing of all the things that were right to do to her feeling. In some ways she was quite pleasing, she was so to her husband, to him she was very pleasing. She was not really pleasing to her brother David Hersland, to him she was not appealing nor domineering and it took women of these two kinds to be pleasing to him, but he knew she was a good woman who would always do what was right for her to do to her feeling, and mostly he thought she was right in her feeling and in her way of doing what was right to her feeling and so he was willing that she should choose a wife to content him.

Martha's husband had a cousin who had once worked for old Mr. Hissen. This cousin of Martha's husband who had come to see a good deal of them tried to arrange a marriage between his brother and another of the Hissen sisters, one of the pleasantest of them. It was a good chance for her for the brother of the cousin was a very well to do man and he was a good enough man though a very stupid and a dull one. It was a good chance for one of them and this one, one of the pleasantest ones of them was willing to meet him but seeing him set her off laughing and every time she saw him again she went on laughing and at last he grew angry and that was the end of her marrying.

But now there was a chance for the marrying of another one of them, of Fanny Hissen and she was soon now to meet David Hersland and to see whether she would be pleasing to him, to make a wife to him to content him.

Martha had come to know them well enough to see them fairly often. She was pleasing to the old man Hissen. She was a sensible good woman and always neat in her dressing. She was not afraid of him. She had a kind of sentimental feeling and that made her respect the Hissen religion, she had a hard way of thinking and that made her like the gentleness of all the pleasant Hissen women, she had a kind of a common feeling and that made her respect the old Hissen woman who spent her life in sorrowing, in weeping out the sadness of all living. And yet always Martha had the important feeling, she knew what was the right way to do to keep on living, to help people to marrying, to make the world keep on as it was in the beginning.

To the Hissen women this Martha was always a little common. But they were wrong in their feeling. This Martha was not really inside her even a little common, it was her hard way of thinking that gave the Hissen women such a feeling. It was that she did not have in her any fine feeling. All the Hissen men and women had fine feeling. This Martha did not have any fine feeling but she was not common in her feeling. Any way the Hissen girls who were coming now to be women and who began to feel in them the liking to have men choose them to content them, were very willing to let this Martha do what they could not do themselves with the finer kind of feeling they all had in them. Not that Martha ever had a common match making feeling or ever wanted to do anything except just what it was right for her to do to her feeling.

And so it came that she chose Fanny Hissen to be the one that should be married to her brother David Hersland who needed now to have a wife to content him, to go to Gossols with him, to help him in his living, to have children for him so that the world could go on as it had from the beginning.

Martha was in a way common to them. David never gave any one of them any such a feeling. He was as big as all the world in his beginning and low and high and noisy and delicate it was all in him, he was it, they were in him and low things were big in him so that no one could ever feel them in him as low things inside him, no never not even when he was an old man and things were falling down inside him and around him in his being.

Soon now then Fanny Hissen was married to David Hersland and went out to Gossols with him, and now together they were to begin their living, to make children who perhaps would come to have in them a really important feeling of themselves inside them.

Mrs. Fanny Hersland had always had in her the beginning of an almost important feeling which she had from being like her mother in her nature, the mother who had had, in her sad trickling arising of itself inside her, an almost important feeling. This beginning of an almost important feeling, had never in Fanny Hissen been very real inside her while she was living in Bridgepoint, for then the strongest thing in her was the family way of being and that always would have been just so strong in her and it never would have come to her to have any realer feeling of being important to herself inside her if she had not gone to Gossols and left the family way of being behind her. It was not marrying that gave her such a feeling. Marrying would never have changed her from the family way of being, it was going to Gossols and leaving the family being and having a for her unnatural way of living that awoke in her a sense inside her of the almost important feeling that was to come to be inside her.

It had its beginning with her knowing, in the hotel where the Herslands were living before they settled down in the ten acre place, it had its beginning with her knowing old Mrs. Schilling and her daughter Sophie Schilling and her other daughter Pauline Schilling. With them there began inside her a sense of individual being, not that it was different in her to her feeling, it was only different in her being.

When one just met with them, old flabby Mrs. Schilling and her daughter the fat Sophie Schilling and the other daughter the thinner Pauline Schilling, they were at first meeting and even after longer knowing like many other ordinary women. Yet always one had a little uncertain feeling that perhaps each one of them had something queer in her. One could never be very certain with them whether this possible queerness of them was because of something queer inside in all them or that they were queer because something had been left out in each one of them in the making of them or that they had lost something out of them that should have been inside in them. Mostly they were just ordinary stupid enough women like millions of them.

The mother was one of those fat heavy women who are all straight down the front of them when they are sitting. When they are walking they are always slowly waddling with heavy breathing.

Many such fat flabby waddling women have something queer about them. These have big doughy empty heads on top of them. These heads on them give to one a kind of feeling such as a baby's head gives to one in the first months of its being living, that the head is not well fastened to them, that it will fall off them if one does not hold it together on them. They have been living, working, cooking, directing, they have been chosen by a man to content him, they have had children come into the world through them, sometimes strong men and women have been born from inside them, they have made marriages for their children and managed people around them, they have lived and suffered and some of them have had power in them, and they are flabby now with big doughy heads that wobble on them.

Old Mrs. Schilling was such a one.

The fat daughter Sophie Schilling was a little like her mother but her head was not yet wobbly on her.

They seemed to have enough money to live comfortably in the hotel together. They had a poodle dog who was company for the mother. They never quarrelled with each other. They did not have any troubles there at the hotel where they were comfortably living together.

It was a month or so after the Herslands had come to the hotel that Mrs. Hersland began to know Sophie Schilling. She had met her going about in the hotel and sometimes when she was out she met with her and they came in together. They soon began to call on each other. Mrs. Hersland began to know the mother and the sister Pauline Schilling. It is easy to see how the knowing Sophie Schilling and her mother and the sister Pauline Schilling would awaken in her the always possible almost important feeling that was quiet until then inside her.

Sophie Schilling never meant very much to her. They were very much together and Fanny Hersland always felt for her. She had no affection for her and after she moved away from the hotel she did not very often see her.

The year that they both lived in the hotel they were a great deal together but Sophie did not impress her, she never became really important to her, Mrs. Hersland had not really any affection for her. Mrs. Hersland never came any nearer to the mother, and the sister Pauline Schilling.

Knowing Sophie Schilling and her mother and her sister was really very important to her. They were a problem to her.

One never learnt anything about them or against them, nobody gossiped about them, there were plenty of people who knew them and came to see them. Each one of them had their own friends and they always got along very nicely with them, only somehow there was always there this emptiness they had in them. It was a hole that each one had inside in her. And so one could not come to any certain judgement of them, one could never be sure about them, that they had something queer inside them, or that they were all three of them just like the many millions who have been made just like them.

It is easy to see how this puzzling quality of them would awaken in Mrs. Hersland who was almost always now with them, the always possible almost important feeling that was quiet until then inside her. She always had a feeling for Sophie Schilling but she had no affection for her, Sophie was not in any way important to her, Mrs. Hersland never came to feel any nearer to the mother and the sister Pauline Schilling. She never came to feel certain about them inside her and this not being certain of the kind of judgement which was natural to her, made a beginning inside her of an almost individual feeling, different in her, but not different to her, from the family way of being which had always until then been all there was of living to her.

After leaving the hotel she never saw much of them. Occasionally she would call on them to show her children. All the Schilling women were always good to them but they were never important to them, there came to be soon very little visiting between them and then very soon there was none. This was the end of the beginning in Mrs. Hersland of the possible almost important feeling.

Always now it kept on growing, a little from her husband and making him do things through her compelling, but mostly from her dependents, the governesses seamstresses servants and the others, the for her poor queer people who soon came to be always around her.

The loving David Hersland had in him for his wife was that in some ways she was a flower to him, in some ways just a woman to him. He needed a woman to content him. The power she had in her sometimes over him was not important to him, that was only a joke to him, what was real in her to him was that sometimes she was a flower to him and mostly she was just a woman to content him.

Men outside him awoke in him, a need almost always in him, to fight with them. Women could never give him any such feeling to have inside him. If they had a power in them, he would brush them away from around him, sometimes with men outside him he would in the same way brush them away from before him, but they often then would be stubborn things around him, he could not brush them away from him; but all women to him, if he needed to brush them away from around him, he could so always rid himself of them. If a woman held her power in him it was because of brilliant seductive managing, and so there would not be aroused in him any desire of fighting nor of brushing her away from him. His wife was different to him, she was appealing there inside him like a tender feeling he had in him. Often she was not important to him, often she was not even existing to him. Sometimes, and this was the rarest thing in him, she filled for him a need to have a sense of beauty in him, then she was like a flower to him, but this did not happen very often in him, more often she had a kind of power over him that was only a joke to him, mostly in their daily living the power she had in her with him did not to himself touch him, it was her managing to have things for the children, to have her way in small things, sometimes in a big one, but these things never were important to him, and he never knew she felt a power in them, the only power he knew she felt over him was only a joke to him, it could never have any other meaning to him, and that was all there was of the effect she had upon him.

He did not need now when he was still a vigorous man and strong in his living, he did not need to have a woman to complete him, he needed a woman only to be pleasing, he needed a woman only to content him. This perhaps would come to be different in him when he would be an old man and weakening, then perhaps a woman who had power in her for him, a power to hold him by seductive managing, such a woman could then fill up in him empty places made by old age and his weakening and his shrinking away from the outside of him, he would need such a one then to complete him. Now he was a strong man and vigorous in his living and such a woman could arouse him but he would not need to have her in him and he would, when she was too much with him, for he met her often enough in his living, he would brush her away from before him.

They were living, the father the mother and the three children, there had been two other children but they had died in the beginning, they were living then the five of them and the servants and governesses and dependents they had with them, in the ten acre place in that part of Gossols where no other rich people were living. Here they lived a life that was not the natural way of being for them here they had around them only, for them, poor queer kind of people and these came to be for them all the people they had in their daily living. More and more there was no visiting for them with the richer people who were the natural people for them to have as friends around them. The father spent his days with rich men for he had his business with them, he was making his great fortune among them, but more and more his wife lived with the poorer people who were living right around them, more and more his wife in her daily living had all of her being in her relation to the servants seamstresses governesses with whom she was living and she was always of them and always was above them and in the same way she was with them the poor, for her, queer people around her.

There were then the three children, Martha, Alfred and David, there was the father of them and they all three of them more and more had a fear in them of him and all of them more and more mostly were in opposition to him. There was the mother of them and she was never very important to any one of them, she was not as important to any one of them as she was to the father of them for the little power she had in her was always a pleasant joke to him. Then there were the servants, the governesses and the dependents and the people who lived near them, who soon were all that the three of them had as people to be in their daily living.

The occasional visiting to the part of Gossols where the richer people were living had never much of reality to them. Visiting with their mother came to be harder for all three of them when they were beginning to be self conscious and a little older. When they were very little ones six years and younger there was a little pleasure in visiting with their mother. Then it began to be harder, they would shrink behind the mother, they got a little pleasure from the smell of fur and silk that they got as they shrank closer to her, they got a little pleasure from the smell of beaver that they had from the best hats they wore when they went with her but that was all there was of pleasure, more and more as they grew older they almost hated the people who lived in that part of Gossols where people were richer, where they were made by them, these children and the mothers of them, where they were made by them to have discomfort by their not knowing how to act when they came together. So more and more they would not go with their mother.

The mother never knew it of them that her children were not comfortable with well to do children and the mothers of them because of the living that was not the natural way of living for them. It never could come to be a real thing to her that she was cut off from right rich living.

It was then slowly coming to be true of them that the children were more entirely of them, the poorer people who lived around them, than they were of their mother then, than their mother was of them then though they were all that there was of their mother's daily living. To the mother of them they were to the people around them as she was to them, of them and above them in her right well to do city being, it never could come to her to feel that the three children who were to her feeling inside to her as they had been when she bore them were in all their being all in common with the life they were daily leading with all of them who were around them.

There were many kinds of people then living around them. Some of them were sometimes working for them, dress-making carpentering shoe-mending, odd jobs were done by some of them. They were very many of them then the poorer people who were living around them, there were very many of them and they were all of them in each one of them then different from all the others of them and this all three of the children knew very well inside them.

There were many people living in small houses around them. Some of them were families of women, some of them were made up of some good ones and some who were not good to earn a living, there were families where it was a little hard to understand how they were living, nobody did any working, nobody had money that belonged to them. In some of the families around them there was a father who was really not very existing, no one was certain that he was a husband of the woman and the father of the children who all earned the living, such a one would just come and eat and sleep in the house with them, with some there was no mother and one was not very certain from anything the father showed in him or that the children remembered about him that there had ever been one. All that was existing for any of them were the things that happened to them.

In several of the families around them the father or a son had mysterious things he was doing every day in his earning of his living then. Mostly there was nothing bad in any of them, one of them had an intelligence office where he was working, none of his family ever liked to talk about him, it is often so with the work men do to earn a living, there is nothing bad about them, there is nothing in the work that is wrong that gives a reason why they should not do it then to earn their living, they do it every day and earn a living then but somehow it is a feeling the family have about him that they never talk as if he were of them.

All of them who lived near the ten acre place where the Herslands were living in that part of Gossols where no other rich people were living all of them then were good enough people and regular enough in their daily living and mostly all of the families of them had lived a long enough time where they were living then. Mostly they were honest enough working men and women and their children went to school and went on to be decent enough men and women to go on living as their families always had been living.

As I was saying they were very different each one of them from the others of them, each family of them from all the other families of them. There was one family of them that was a family of women then, there was a father to them and he was not dead then or living away from them but mostly then it was as far as one could know a family of women, a mother and there were three daughters then Anna and Cora and Bertha.

The mother's face was old now and a little wooden. She was a foreign woman. She was a hard-working woman, she did dress-making, she earned a good enough living, they were doing very well with their living all of them then. There was nothing in her to connect her with the past the present or the future, there was not any history of her. She had existence in her like the useful things around her, she had character, she had had changes in her and now she was getting older and there was a little more wooden change inside her and so there would be changes in her until she would be all through with all the changes she had in her and always there would be real existence to her and always there would be character to her always there would never be a past or present or a future connected with her, always there would be existence in her, there would be changes, there would never be any history of her to her.

The eldest daughter of them Anna had come then to be a rather beautiful woman. No one thought it about them that all three of them would have that as a change in them. No one thought it about her the mother of them that she had had once a change in her like this change in them before she had borne any of them. The eldest one had beauty then, now when she was grown to be a woman, all three of them one after the other came to have in them as one of the changes that went through them, beauty in them when they were not any longer children.

There were many other families then living in the little houses near the ten acre place where the Hersland family were living in that part of Gossols where no other rich people were living, some of them were neat and made a good living like this family of women, some were not so well off in their living, some had a very straggling way of living, each one of the families of them in the small houses then had each its own way each its own uncertain ways of being, and this is a history of them.

One of these families then was made up of a father and two children, a boy and a girl Eddy and Lilly and the father of them, there were many uncertain things about all three of them, about the living that they had had before in them, about there not being to them a woman to be a wife to him and a mother to the two children, about the way they had money to live on when not any one of the three of them did any working, about the kind of man the father was for it was very hard to know anything about him, about the character of the two children; one thing was certain about them, they had religion in them, they were important in religion.

The father was a tall thin man, they said of him that he was a sick man, perhaps that was true of him, no one knew how anybody knew that about him, his children never said it of him, he was a tall thin blond man, he was always smoking and that was said by every one who knew him to be because it was good for him, he was important in religion.

To the father Mr. Richardson religion was like eating and sleeping and washing, all these and religion made him a continuous being, they were not outside him, they all were in him and they made him always continue in his existing.

Washing is very common, almost everyone does some washing, with some it is only for cleansing, with some it is a refreshing, with some a ceremonial thing that makes them important to every one who knows them. Eating and sleeping are not like loving and breathing. Washing is not like eating and sleeping. Believing is like breathing and loving. Religion can be believing, it can be like breathing, it can be like loving, it can be like eating or sleeping, it can be like washing. It can be something to fill up a place when some one has lost out of them a piece that it was natural for them to have in them.

Mr. Richardson had always had, from his beginning, religion in him. There were some who did not understand it in him, who thought it of him that religion was in him as a kind of lying but these did not understand religion in him, it was in him and had been in him from his beginning, it was in him as eating was in him, as sleeping was in him, as washing was to him. It did not make him important to himself inside him, it did make him important to every one that knew him.

This father Mr. Richardson and his two children Eddy and Lilly were different from any of the others who lived then in the small houses near the ten acre place where the Hersland family were living in that part of Gossols where no other rich people were living. Slowly the Hersland children came to know the three of them, they began to know then the character of the two children Eddy and Lilly Richardson, they never came to have in them, the Hersland family then, much more knowledge of the father of the two children Mr. Richardson.

There were then many families living in the small houses near the ten acre place where the Hersland family were living then in that part of Gossols where no other rich people were living. They were, all of them, more and more interesting to the three Hersland children as these came always more and more to know them, as they came more and more to be a part of them.

To begin again then when it was slowly coming to be true of them that the three children were more entirely of them, the poorer people who lived around them, than they were of their mother then, than their mother was of them then, though they were all there was of their mother's daily living then.

They were all there was of their mother's daily living then but they were nothing to her then of the important being that was beginning to be strong inside her then. They were to her in her then as they had been when she was bearing them, they were part of her as her arms or heart were part of her then, she felt them, she took care of them then as she took care of her body out of which she had once made them and so she always felt them. Later she was lost among them, she would be scared then and they were no longer of her then, they were not any longer in her then to her. Those who always after remembered about her were the servants, the governesses, the dependents who had been around her, they always were a real life to her, they were the important feeling in her, they always remembered about her, they had felt the real important being to herself inside her.

They were all living, this family then, in a pleasant house in a ten acre place where living was very pleasant for them. They did there a little fancy farming, they had a little grain and fruit trees and vegetable gardening, they had many kinds of trees and sometimes they chopped down one of them, they had dogs and chickens and sometimes ducks and turkeys in the yard then, they had horses and two cows and sometimes they had young ones from the horses and the cows and that was very interesting to all of them, sometimes they had rabbits and always they had dogs, often they had a number of men working for them to get the hay in, sometimes they would catch rats and mice in the barn and that was very exciting to the children and sometimes to the father of them, and all around the ten acre place to shut all these joys in was a hedge of roses and in the summer many people came to pick them and then the family would let the dogs loose to bark at them and scare them, sometimes some one would come at night to steal fruit from them sometimes to steal a chicken and then there would be excitement for all of them and the dogs would be let loose to find the man but the dogs then were mostly not very anxious to get into danger with a strange man, they barked hard and that was all the danger there was for them or for the man who was stealing.

All three of the children were beginning to have in them their own individual feeling. This began early in each one of them as it mostly is with children who have freedom in them and a father full up with beginning to commence them. They were different each one of them from the others of them in the troubles they had then inside them, in the lonely feeling they had sometimes in them that each one was alone inside and this was sometimes all they needed to content them. Each one of them was very different inside from the others of them, in all their ways each one of them had different feelings from the others of them different ways of being alone inside in them, different ways of thinking feeling suffering and playing.

As I was saying life was regular enough for all of them for the three children and the father and the mother of them. The children went to public school for their education. Their father had ideas about other things they should learn, other ways of doing besides the ways of the other children around them and it was in such things that he was always beginning. Then there was their eating and their doctoring and the father always had new ideas inside him, new ways of beginning in ways they should have of eating and the doctoring that was good for children.

All three of them had many kinds of education because of him. Sometimes all three would be having just ordinary schooling. Sometimes all three would be having extra teaching, sometimes one or the other stopped going to school to try some other way of education that their father then thought would be good then for that one of them. Sometimes their father would be strong in religion and then this would make for the children complications in their daily living.

They had some troubles with him then in their early living, sometimes in ways of doctoring, sometimes when he thought it was good for all of them to have castor oil given to them, sometimes when he thought a chinese doctor would be good for them, sometimes when he had a queer blind man to examine some one of them.

Sometimes in little things it would be annoying to them in their early living, his way of beginning and then never knowing that he was full up with impatient feeling and so had stopped and wanted others to keep on going. Sometimes this would be annoying of an evening. He would want to play cards and the three of them would begin with him, to please him. The children felt it to be hard on them when they would have begun playing cards just to oblige him and after a few minutes with them he would have arise in him his impatient feeling, and he would say, "here you just finish it up I haven't time to go on playing," and he would call the governess to take his hand from him and all three of the children would have then to play together a game none of them would have thought of beginning, and they had to keep on going for often he would stop in his walking to find which one was winning, and it never came to him to know that he had made the beginning and that the children were playing just because they had to, for him. It was a small thing but it happened very often to them and it was annoying for them.

Real country living feeling all three of the Hersland children in their younger living had inside them, a real country living feeling. This they had in them in the ten acre place with the hired men working and the chickens and ducks and fruit-trees and haymaking and seed-sowing and cows and some vegetable gardening.

The three children had in many ways then in them the feeling of real country living. Their mother never had this feeling, with her it was always country house city living. In the children it was sometimes a real country living feeling that they had in them, and they were then very really a part of the life around them, of country ways of making a living, of cows and chickens and fruit-trees and hunting, and it was for them then in their younger living not country house city living, it was for them then real country living and country feeling and village life around them and hard-working country ways of earning a living.

With the people living in the small houses near them Mr. Hersland mostly had in him city country house living, he was important to all of them, the only rich man in that part of Gossols where they were living. He had it in him to feel other things inside him, sometimes to feel in him a real country living feeling, sometimes he brushed it all away from him, the country feeling, the city country house feeling living, he was then inside him a city man with city schemes and troubles and men around him, and then he walked up and down and his impatient feeling was irritable inside him and he would be muttering and talking to himself and jingling the money in his pockets then and more and more it came to be true of him that he walked up and down thinking, to himself inside him working, scheming, brushing men away from around him, domineering over them, going another way not knowing inside him that he was leaving them because they were then too many for him.

More and more in their later living in the ten acre place in that part of Gossols where no other rich people were living there was for him no reality to country living, to city country house living. For the people around them then in Mrs. Hersland then it was rich city country house living, in Mr. Hersland city being, in the three Hersland children each one a mixed thing in them of the three ways of feeling, rich city country house being country being and city being, and the mixtures of these three feelings in each one of the three of them to the people in the small houses near them is part of the history of each one of the three of them.

Each one of them had something in them then of real country feeling. They got it in many ways, in hay-making, hay cutting, helping the men working, eating bread and vegetables, fruit as they were picking it, they got it from milking, and butter and cheese making, they got it from the seasons and the things they did to help things growing, they got it in every way around them, they got it in helping ploughing, they got it from playing Indians and having darkness come around them, they got it from eating grass and leaves and having the taste in their mouths to bring back such things to them in their later living, they got it in every kind of way then. They got it from the feeling of the wind around them, when they shouted with it around them, when they crouched down somewhere with it cut off from them, when they helped the men sowing seed with it blowing around them, and when the trees hit their own wood and made that queer sound that they got to have inside them. One can only get the real feeling of wind blowing in the country, in country living. Strong wind blowing needs real country living to give it a right feeling and this they all three of them each in their own way had then inside them.

Real country living feeling all three of the Hersland children in their younger living had inside them, a real country living feeling. In their later living it was differ-ent in each one of them. In Martha this being part of the country village living was not in her later living inside her to her feeling but it was inside her in her being. In Alfred there was in his later living nothing of this in him, not in his being not in his feeling; he was of his mother then, the feeling she had had in her was what was in him then, the being important to himself inside her, the having in her the right rich being which was the natural being in her. In the younger brother David this early living was made by him into him as he made all his living in him, he made it a part of him, it was something in him to be made over inside him to be a part of the whole of him.

In their younger living all the three children Martha, Alfred and David, all of them had it in them to be more or less afraid of their father when he was angry or even playing with them. This was more or less true then of all three of them. Later in their living when it had come to be with him that he was full up with impatient feeling, that then there was nothing in him that was not impatient feeling, then they had not any longer much fear of him, they knew it then about him that he was filled up with impatient feeling, they knew then that the anger in him never would drive him to any last act against them. Martha had always a little left in her even in his latest living of this fear of him, Alfred and David then had no fear of him, they could stand up to him and win out against him with not any fear inside them of where his anger might drive him.

There are many kinds of men and there are many millions made of each kind of them. Of the kind that Mr. David Hersland was he had a great deal of it in him, later it all turned into impatient feeling inside him, later then it became only a weakness in him, he was shrunk away from the outside of him, he needed others then inside him to fill him.

There are many kinds of men then and there are always many millions made of each kind of them. David Hersland had a mixture in him and this will come out clearly in the history of him. One can never know certainly in any one the nature of him when he is a boy or a young man for then there are many things to drive him that are not the nature of him, in the middle living it is only the nature in him that will drive him and this will come out then always more and more in him as he begins then at the beginning of the ending of his middle living to repeat more and more the whole of him.

A man in his living has many things inside him. Men in their living have many things inside them, they have in them, each one of them has it in them, his own way of feeling himself important inside him, they have in them all of them their own way of beginning, their own way of ending, their own way of working, their own way of having loving inside them and having loving come out of them, their own way of having anger inside them and letting their anger come out from inside them, their own way of eating, their on way of drinking, their own way of sleeping, their own way of doctoring. They have each one of them their own way of fighting, they have in them all of them their own way of having fear in them. They have all of them in them their own way of believing, their own way of being important inside them, their own way of showing to others around them the important feeling inside in them.

There are then many kinds of men and many millions of each kind of them. In many men there is a mixture in them, there is in them the bottom nature in them of their kind of men the nature that makes their kind of thinking, their kind of eating, of drinking and of loving, their kind of beginning and ending, there is then in many men this bottom nature in them of their kind of men and there is mixed up in them the nature of other kinds of men, natures that are a bottom nature in other men and makes of such men that kind of man.

Some men have it in them in their loving to be attacking, some have it in them to let things sink into them, some let themselves wallow in their feeling and get strength in them from the wallowing they have in loving, some in loving are melting — strength passes out from them, some in their loving are worn out with the nervous desire in them, some have it as a dissipation in them, some have it as excitement in them, some have it as a clean attacking, some have it in them as a daily living — some as they have eating in them, some as they have drinking, some as they have sleeping in them, some have it in them as believing, some have it as a simple beginning feeling — some have it as the ending always of them such of them are always old men in their loving.

Men and women have in them many ways of living, — their ways of eating, their ways of drinking, their ways of thinking, their ways of working, their way of sleeping, in most men and many women go with the way of loving, come from the bottom nature in them.

David Hersland had a mixture in him. His wife was in him in his early middle living she was in him then as a tender feeling, when she was outside of him to him she was a little joke to him, mostly she was not when outside him then important to him, later she was a little important to him because of the children and her resistance to him for them, then a little more and more then there changed in him a feeling of her being a joke to him to his brushing her away from around him, less and less then she was in him as a tender feeling, less and less then she was important to him. Mr. David Hersland had in him a feeling of being as big as all the world around him, he had in him a strong feeling of beginning, of fighting of brushing people away from around him, of hearty laughing, in his middle living of pleasant every day living in his country house living.

Mrs. Hersland had in her different ways of having herself inside her, of having important feeling in her. A feeling of herself inside her would never have come to be in her if she had gone on living in the way that was natural for her. Being important to herself inside her first came to be a little in her from the knowing Sophie Schilling and her sister Pauline Schilling and the mother Mrs. Schilling, later it came to be stronger in her from the living with the governesses and seamstresses and servants and dependents and being with them but above them all the time every moment of her living, not cut off to her feeling but really cut off in her living from the rich living that was for her the natural way of being.

She had then in her, in her middle living it was strongest in her, a feeling of herself to herself inside her. Once this came to be in her almost a lonesome feeling inside her but it was not real enough in her, it did not come enough of itself from inside her, it never came to be altogether really a lonesome feeling in her.

There are very many ways for women to have loving in them, some have loving in them for any one or anything that needs them, some have loving in them from the need in them for some other one or for something they see around them, some have a mixture in them. There are some who have really not any loving in them. The kinds of loving women have in them and the way it comes out from them makes for them the bottom nature in them, makes them their kind of women and there are always many millions made of each kind of them.

Mrs. Hersland then was of the kind of women who have resisting in them only with a feeling of themselves inside them, Mrs. Hersland was of the kind of women who have dependent independence in them, Mrs. Hersland was of the kind of women, though she had this to be in her so timidly inside her so gently within her that mostly nobody ever knew it to themselves about her, she had it in her to be of the kind of women to own those they need for loving, to subdue anyone who needs them to be important to them.

In their middle living in that part of Gossols where no other rich people were living the Hersland family had with them only women in the house with them. They had had then mostly in their living german women as servants in the house with them, sometimes they could not get them, once they had an Irishwoman, twice Italian women, once a Mexican. The Irish woman and one of the Italian women had a little queerness in them, the queerness that comes from being a servant and cooking and sitting alone in a kitchen and having a mistress to direct them and sometimes children to tease them, these had to be sent away all of a sudden.

Some women have it in them to be in all their living children, to have a childish nature in them all through their living. Some men have such a thing always in them, mostly men have it in them more than women to have in all their living a little childish nature in them. Some women have it in them all their living to have a grimy little girl nature in them, some have it in them to have a little girl sweet shrinking little lying nature always in them. Some women have it in their living to have in them a being just before adolescent living, to have in them all through their living the fear of coming adolescence about beginning, in them, these always have it in them to be very lively so as to keep adolescence from giving sorrow to them, these have not in them senti-mental feeling, they have aggressive liveliness in them. There are some men who have in them all through their living such a nature in them. Some women have all their living their school feeling in them, they never get through, from their beginning to their ending, with such feeling, such being, such living, it is in them and nothing can change them, they are always school girls in their being, some of them always are as school girls in their feeling, some of them always are as school girls in their living, some women have some of this in them all through their living from their beginning to their ending. Some women have it in them and there are always many millions of them and they are to themselves like men in their living there are many women who are always vigorous young women energetic and getting information and busy every moment in their living and sometime there will be a history of many of such of them. Then there are many women who have some kind of woman nature in them and always in the millions of all the kinds of them there is always in them one nature or the other nature in them, there is always some kind or every kind of mixture in them, sometime there will be a history of every one of every kind of them, sometime there will be a history of everyone who ever was or is or will be living, there must always sometime be a history of each one from their beginning to their ending, of every one who ever was or is or will be living. This is now a history of some of them.

As I was saying Mrs. Hersland had mostly in her middle living in Gossols in that part where no other rich people were living, older foreign or foreign american women as servants in the house with them. Once one foreign girl had come to her from some one in Bridgepoint who had sent her because she wanted to go and this friend thought she would be a good servant for Mrs. Hersland to have in the house with her. The girl did not want to stay, she wanted to go back to Bridgepoint, she said Mrs. Hersland should help send her, Mrs. Hersland had then an angry feeling in her, she said she did not have to help send her. The girl said she would have to help a little to send her, Mrs. Hersland said she would either not give her anything to help her or she would pay everything for her, she never would help to send her away from her, she would pay the whole thing for her, it was not right but she would pay the whole thing for her, she would do it all or nothing for her, she did not have to do anything for her, she would do the whole thing for her. Mrs. Hersland had in her a bright angry feeling inside her, it was wrong that a girl should behave so toward her. This was Mrs. Hersland with an injured feeling inside her and an angry feeling then in her. Mostly she would then pay everything any one could in any kind of way ask of her to show them the right angry feeling in her.

Mrs. Hersland was of this kind of them then, she had resisting as her way of being. This is not always clear in the beginning sometimes it is the resisting that is in appearance like attacking, sometimes the attacking that has stubbornness or weakness in it like resisting but more in their living this nature in them comes out of them in the repeating that is in all being. And so always whenever Mrs. Hersland had an injured feeling or an angry feeling in her she did such a thing to satisfy herself inside her.

As I was saying Mrs. Hersland had three seamstresses working for her when she was living in Gossols in her middle living when she was strongest in her feeling of being herself inside her in her living. One of these was living in a part of Gossols between the part where the Herslands were living where no other rich people were living and the part where mostly all the rich people were living. Then she had one who lived in a part nearer where the rich people were living, she went to this one. Then there was the woman who lived in a small house near them, the woman who had the three daughters who all of them sometime had beauty in them.

The one who lived in between always worked twice a year in the fall and in the spring to make dresses for Mrs. Hersland and Martha and sometimes for the governess then living in the house with them. She always came to work in the house with them, she always ate there with them, and sometimes when she was in a hurry to finish her work she remained altogether in the house sleeping and eating. Her name was Lillian Rosenhagen. She was a large woman, she had black hair and she was tall and she had long heavy fingers that were tapering and heavy again just where the nails were commencing. Lillian Rosenhagen was a stupid woman and never said anything but the children could never forget having her in the house with them. She was of the kind of them and there are always many always being made of them who have it in them to be stupid, to be heavy, to be drifting, and yet one never forgets them when one has known them, they do nothing but they have a physical something in them that makes them.

Every kind of history about any one is important then, every kind of way of thinking about any one is important to those who need a whole history of every one.

Lillian Rosenhagen had always repeating in her an anxious feeling, she had very little in her of impatient feeling. As I was saying Lillian Rosenhagen was very good at sewing, she was very steady at working, she had always in her repeating an anxious feeling when she had to do any ending or beginning.

Lillian Rosenhagen never had any man who really wanted to marry her. They all liked her. Mostly every one who knew her liked her. She lived together with her mother and sometimes her sister. The Rosenhagen sisters were both born american. The father was not living. The mother was old then and did nothing but a little cleaning and cooking, the daughter Lillian did most of the supporting of the mother. Sometimes Cecilia would be helping but she never got as much money for working as Lillian and often she was not living with them.

Lillian was four years older than her sister Cecilia. Cecilia had a very unpleasant nature, she had nervousness in her, she had suspicion in her, she had an anxious being as excitement always working in her. She was not a good worker, she was not a bad worker, she could find people to employ her and they would always be ready to keep her longer than her suspicious temper would let her.

Cecilia Rosenhagen was a true spinster. Lillian Rosenhagen was not married because nobody had come to want her enough to take her. These two were very different in nature. There is every kind of being in women who have it in common to have a spinster nature.

So then they went on with their living to their ending Lillian and Cecilia Rosenhagen. No man ever married either one of them. They both went on in their own way living and dress-making to their ending. Mrs. Hersland liked to have Miss Lillian Rosenhagen in the house working. She was a good young woman for dress-making, she never gave to Mrs. Hersland anything of an injured or angry feeling. No man came to ever want to marry her, she went on to her ending living and dress-making and now this is all the history of her.

The other seamstress who did sewing for Mrs. Hersland in her middle living, the one who lived in that part of Gossols where richer people were living, the one that made for Mrs. Hersland then all her best dresses the ones she used for visiting, this woman then was of a kind of woman as I was saying who have in them very little of anxious being or impatient being, sometimes impatient being, a little of angry feeling, sometimes some injured feeling.

So then there was a woman Mary Maxworthing who did dress-making in Gossols and lived in that part of Gossols where richer people were living, there was this woman who had independent dependent being and had in her a certain kind of being and there are always being made many millions of women and there are always being made many millions of men who have in them the same kind of being she had in her in her living. Now there is a history of Mary Maxworthing and her business of dress-making.

Mary Maxworthing then lived her own life, had her own way of dress-making, she was not of them who live other people's lives in living. She was very successful in dress-making, she never earned real distinction, she never in living did really very personal creating but she lived her own life in her living and she had a fairly successful life from her beginning to her ending. She had men who wanted her to marry them, when she was thirty-five she did marry and she married very well then, not well enough to give up dress-making but well enough to be very comfortable in living.

I like to tell it better in a woman the kind of nature a certain kind of men and women have in living, I like to tell it better in a woman because it is clearer in her and I know it better, a little, not very much better. Such a nature as Mary Maxworthing had in her is of the kind of nature that many men and women have in them.

It is very interesting that every one has in them their kind of stupid being. It is very important to know it in each one which part in them, which kind of feeling in them is connected with stupid being in them. Sometime there will be a history of every kind of stupid being in every kind of human being in every part of the living of each one from their beginning to their ending.

Stupid being then is in every one, in some it is with the bottom in them, in some with the other nature or natures in them, in some with the feeling coming out of them. In some it is always repeating, in some it is only rarely repeating, there is every kind of accent in repeating stupid being, sometime there will be a history of all of them.

Mary Maxworthing was one of the children of an american man and woman who had made a good enough living at farming. Their name was changed some in their american living. Mary came to Gossols to work for her living when she was about sixteen. She first earned her living by taking care of children. She did not find this very amusing. She liked children but she wanted freedom. She began to think when she was about twenty-one of some other way of earning a living. She thought over everything, a little dairy to sell butter and eggs and milk and cream but she did not like that kind of work and it takes a great deal of money to begin. She thought of millinering but she was not a very good hand at hat trimming, she was very good at sewing but she knew nothing about cutting and fitting. She was then about twenty-five when she came to this decision, when she decided to do dress-making. So then she sent for her relation Mabel Linker who lived down in the country to come and join her. She went on working at being nursery governess to earn a living for the two of them while Mabel was to learn cutting and fitting and dress-making from the beginning. Mabel Linker was soon very clever at dress-making. Then they started an establishment for dress-making in that part of Gossols where richer people were living. They did not then have success with their undertaking.

They had not enough customers to pay them to keep going, Mary Maxworthing soon used up all the money she had saved up to begin this undertaking, soon then the two of them began quarreling, soon then they had for a while to give up dress-making; Mary had to go back to her place and once more begin to earn a living by taking care of children.

Mabel Linker had very little common sense, she had little twittering flighty ways in her but she was a good sewer, she was a good cutter and fitter, she was almost a brilliant dress-maker, but she had very little stability in her character. Mary Maxworthing began with almost an idolizing of her and then there came trouble when they began living together. Then the money was all gone and they both had become a little bitter. Mary had then almost a despairing feeling in her. Mabel took it all as a thing that had happened to her and now there would be some other thing happen to her. She took it not so much lightly as as a thing that was over and that was all there was about it to her.

Mary Maxworthing had a miserable feeling then in her, she had not an anxious feeling in her because a living for her was always around her, she could always find people to employ her she had this always in her, but she had for the first time in her living in her a discouraged sense of failure.

She and Mabel Linker still continued to live together. Mabel went to work right away for another dress-maker, it was hard work but this did not make really any very great difference to her. For a little while then Mary depended on Mabel Linker to support her, after a little while some one employed her to help out in a little store near her. She stayed there all that summer. Later she went to a friend of the last person who had employed her as a nursery governess for her, and every one who knew her thought that the future now was settled for her.

There are then some kinds of men and women, some men and some women of some kinds of nature who have it in them to have every one who knows them have about the same idea of them. Mary Maxworthing was then such a one. She had a certain gaiety in living but no wildness no recklessness in her being and no one would think such a thing from the certain pleasant gaiety she had in living. She had a little impatient being, a little unpleasant temper in her, a little insistence on interfering in her, a small amount of pride in her, enough of sensitive response to make a reasonable sweetness in her, a little tendency to angry and to injured feeling in her but not very much of this in her not more of this in her than any one would expect from her. She had a reasonable sense of responsibility in her, a reasonable efficiency in her, she was in short what every one thought her.

Mary Maxworthing as I was saying was really what any one who knew her thought her and yet she now had something happen to her that surprised every one who knew her. She was then as I was saying not a very young woman. One day she took a day off to go to the hospital to see a doctor. She went alone not even Mabel Linker was with her.

She went in to the doctor, the doctor asked her a few questions and then examined her, "you know what's the matter with you," he said to her. She grew red, she had a little impatient feeling in her, she had no fear in her and no angry feeling in her. "I don't know what's the matter with me Doctor," was her answer. "You'd better get him to marry you," said the doctor who was angry with her.

There is then stupid being in every one. The doctor was angry with her, "you know what is the matter with you!" he said to her.

She did not then say anything farther, she was not interested in what the doctor had further to say to her. She was through with being stupid in that kind of way of not knowing whether it had really happened to her.

Mary Maxworthing then had a baby in her, it had happened to her and it was a surprise to every one who knew her who learned it about her. Gradually the people who employed her knew what had happened to her. They were surprised too that it could happen to her, she said nothing to explain how it had happened, she said, alright it has happened and she liked children and now she would have one. Every one continued to have the same opinion of her whether they liked her or whether they did not like her as they had had before this happened to her, then every one who knew her had still the same estimate of her.

This is now a history of what now happened to her and how Mabel took care of her, and of Mabel Linker and how they did and did not get along together, and what each one of them felt about the other.

Mary Maxworthing and Mabel Linker were from the same part of the country. They had always known each other. Mary was the elder. Mabel was about five years younger. Mabel Linker's cousin had married Mary Maxworthing's sister. When Mabel came to Gossols to learn dress-making Mary almost idolized her. She liked to write down when she was sitting idling, "Mabel is an angel, angel Mabel," and this showed her feeling.

It was much harder to know it about Mabel Linker what feeling she had in her about any one around her. It was always very hard to know this about her. Perhaps she did not mostly have any very strong feeling in her. When she had a lover it was then certain that she was crazy to have him marry her, she only lived in having him want her. Mostly with every one else around her one never could tell what was the feeling in her.

When Mary came home from the doctor Mabel was told all that had happened to her. Mabel did everything any one could have done for her in all the trouble that then came to her. Everybody was good to her, everybody except the doctor who had got angry with her. He was young then, he thought she had deceit in her, this was not true of her, she was as honest as most people are. I don't mean that she had any great honesty in her. She did not but she had medium honesty in her. In her interview with the doctor there was no deceit in her there was only the stupidity of impatient being in her.

Mabel Linker was working for her living, she had commenced again having work to do in her room and in a small way had commenced again a business of dressmaking though often she had to go out sewing. Mary Maxworthing, when she would have a bad feeling in her, came to Mabel Linker to have her take care of her. Mary had not even then anxious being in her, she did have very much then impatient being in her, it was very hard sometimes for any one to put up with her.

Finally she did not have a living baby, after six months it passed out of her, it was her impatient being in her that made trouble for her, this is a history of what happened to her.

As I was saying Mabel Linker took care of her. It was not an easy matter. She never would go to a doctor. Finally at six months the baby passed out of her. She almost died when this happened to her. Mabel Linker had sent then for a doctor. It came very nearly being too late then to save her. This did not scare her until it was all over. She did not really know what was happening to her. All that happened to her was from the impatient being in her. Impatient being was the stupid being in her.

As I was saying Mary Maxworthing and Mabel Linker were not altogether successful friends in their living. Later they both were married and then things went a little better for them, also they were succeeding then in their business of dress-making. This was when Mrs. Hersland knew them, when they were again living and dress-making in that part of Gossols where rich people were living.

The idolizing feeling in Mary Maxworthing for Mabel Linker did not change into something else in her. It just died out of her. But Mabel really only needed the man who married her, Mabel never wanted anything else to come to her. Later with her husband to urge her she got to have more feeling for a future, she wanted then for him and for herself too then success in dress-making. Mary had some money then and they began again in that part of Gossols where rich people were living.

As I was saying when Mary Maxworthing was looking to a future with freedom and a dress-making undertaking and a little distinction, she had in her a sense of herself to herself inside her, she had in her a sense of living in her, she had something of individual being in her. She had then for Mabel Linker almost an idolizing feeling, this was important feeling in her. Then came the time when she was no longer hoping for the future, then there was some bitterness in her, then she felt Mabel should have more grateful feeling in her than she showed toward her, then came the despairing being in her and then the thing happened to her that surprised every one who knew her when her weakness and desire were more active in her because gaiety and impatient being and ambition were then dead in her. Then when that was over Mary knew how near she had come to be dying, then she had a little anxious impatient irritable being in her and then she and Mabel still lived together and then they quarrelled more and more with each other for Mabel was beginning then with her lover and so she had then the beginning of wanting to escape, a little, in her.

Things then were always getting more and more unpleasant between them. Mary Maxworthing had injured feeling in her, she had impatient being then in her, she was always scolding, she wanted Mabel not to have such flightiness in her, she wanted to keep her from marrying. Mabel then had escaping being in her and she would then sometimes answer and it was then a continued biting chatter whenever they were together and they were always together, they could not keep away from one another. Finally things got so bitter between them that Mary would have nothing further to do with her. Mabel could marry and then when sickness and trouble would come to her she would know better. She told her then to get another machine to sew on, that one was hers and she needed it now for herself and Mabel could go to her lover's family and get them to give one to her, she thought they were such nice people, let them show her. Then Mabel's lover's mother made Mabel promise not to invite Mary Maxworthing to their wedding and that was for some time the end of any relation between them. Mabel Linker then was married and she and her husband had a happy enough existence. The husband's family had to help them and then his mother died and then when Mabel met Mary they began to say "how do you do", again to one another. Later she and Mary got to be friendly again together. Mary had a little money left to her and with Mabel's husband to urge Mabel they began again a business of dress-making in that part of Gossols where rich people were living. Mary Maxworthing did the managing and the fashion and the excusing and the matching and the arranging for fittings and the arranging for paying and the changing, and Mabel the dress--making. They always had some trouble but this time they were successful enough in their undertaking.

These then were the dress-makers Mrs. Hersland had in her middle living. The woman with the daughters, to do plain sewing and making over and putting on skirt braids and sometimes mending. Lillian Rosenhagen to make ordinary dresses for Mrs. Hersland and dresses for Martha and sometimes for the governess living in the house with her, and Mary Maxworthing and Mabel Linker to make her best dresses for her and once to make a dress for the last governess Miss Madeleine Wyman and there is now soon to be a history of this dress for her.

These then made Mrs. Hersland's clothes and clothes for her daughter Martha, sometimes for the governess living with her.

There were, as I was saying, in the middle living of the Hersland family, three governesses, a foreign woman, and a tall blond foreign american who later married a baker, and then Madeleine Wyman who was with them when Mrs. Hersland had in living, her most important feeling.

The first governess then was a foreign woman. She was a good musician. She was then a woman nearly forty. She had been a governess ever since she was twenty. She had been, the last ten years, in America. She had brought her young sister with her, she wanted her to be educated to be a teacher, she wanted her to live in America where life would be easier. She herself did not like it in America, she wanted to go back to her old living where people spoke french and german and where it was natural for her to be a musician. She did not stay very long with the Herslands, her sister soon got a position as teacher and then the elder sister left her, she wanted then to leave America, this did not come to her, she got as far as Cincinnati and then somehow she never got farther. She stayed there and she gave music lessons and she never got any further and she stayed there always until she died there, and she never had left America. She had been ten years in America, she had not much gaiety in living, she had not in her anything of dreary being.

It is then very interesting always to know the stupid being in each one. It was hard to see it in this one. It was hard even to see it in her living with her sister and in this way it often comes out in women. It was hard to know the stupid being in her for no one came close to her not even her sister.

They liked her well enough, the Herslands, when she was governess to them but she made no impression on any of them. She did not give to Mrs. Hersland any important feeling of herself to herself inside her, to her feeling. Mr. Hersland had a theory of her in the beginning, he wanted to have a real foreign woman, a real governess with concentrated being, with german and french and who was really a musician. Theoretically, she was important to him, really she had no existence for him. Then when she left them after a little while with them because her sister had become a teacher and so she could leave her and she wanted to leave America, when she left them Mr. Hersland thought it was better that the children should have american training. They were american, they did not need french and german, they did not need to bother about music then, they could do that later, now they needed strength and gymnastics and out of door living, and swimming and shooting. And that was the end of the first governess for all of them.

They sometimes saw the sister Olga who was a teacher in Gossols but she never talked much about her sister Martha. The children liked Olga, they liked her, they liked to tease her. Mr. Hersland gave her good advice, when Mr. Hersland noticed her he was attracted by her. Olga was very different from her sister Martha.

No one who knew her would think of her as a woman of a spinster nature. She was round and pleasant and men liked her and she had constant attacking ways in her to give to her more attraction and men could be in love with her and she wanted to have attention from them and she made them when they were anywhere near her give it to her, made them sure of her from her actions toward them and she had as a bottom a vague being and later this was in her as nervous being in her, never as impatient being in her.

No one would think of her as a woman with a spinster nature but this was true of her. Always she had attacking in all kinds of ways to give to herself more attraction and always she had as a bottom a vague being so that she was always being baffling, always making for herself a stupid escaping, sometimes not an easy escaping, sometimes she had to escape by accusation. Mrs. Hersland always kept track of her and was good to her.

There was then in the Hersland middle living this first governess who did not stay long with them. As I was saying when Mr. Hersland employed her, he was the one who interviewed her, she was the ideal for him. He wanted a real governess, a foreign woman with governess training, one who was a good musician, one who would talk french and german with the children. When she left he had already in him a new beginning. And so this next governess was very different from the last.

She was a tall blond woman. She had no queerness in her. Later she married a baker. She was a healthy person. There was no trouble for any one to know her stupid being. But it made no difference to any one that she had stupid being, that that was almost her whole being, there was nothing that any one wanted of her that made her stupid being a trouble in her. Stupid being was the whole of her. It was alright in her. It was not actively pleasant in her. It was just all of her.

She was not a music teacher, she had no french or german in her, she just knew the ordinary things and not very well either. There are some, there are many of many kinds of men and women who give to every one the same feeling about them, Mary Maxworthing in her way was such a one. The second governess the Herslands had was a very different kind of such a one. Every one who knew her had the same estimate of her. The children laughed at her, they neither liked or disliked her, Mrs. Hersland had not any feeling about her. Later this one married a baker. He was a big blond man, and they got on well together. She had children, she grew a little larger, her face was thinner, she was a little dirtier then, not very much busier, she never surprised any one who knew her. She married and sometimes later the children of Mrs. Hersland or Mr. Hersland would see her, she was a little grimier then, but nothing was changed in her, she was a little larger, her face and neck were thinner, she and the baker were satisfied with each other.

Mr. David Hersland had in him a feeling of being as big as all the world around him. He had his ideas of educating children. He had seen the first governess they had and he had had a feeling in him that was the ideal governess for his children. He talked to her in the beginning often about them and his rules and wishes for them. Then she made no impression on him, she was not evident enough in the family living to attract his attention. Soon he forgot about the children and their education. Then she left them. Then he was angry with the children that they knew so little french and german.

Then there was in him a new beginning, he thought it better for their english that they should forget all the french and german the first governess had taught them. He wanted a big healthy woman who knew all about farming. The second governess then was such a one. Her mother and father had a dairy farm and she was a big blond woman and she had red cheeks and she was not a musician and she did not know any french and german and she had had only an ordinary education and she knew nothing about spending her time reading. There was no question that she was the ideal Mr. Hersland had then in him for a governess for his children.

He never forgot about her altogether as he did about the first one. She was always some one to him, he liked big healthy women, she did not know much about farming but she listened while he talked to her about farming and about the children. Later when she was married to the baker he would drop in to see her and eat a cake while he talked to her.

Mr. Hersland then had his own way of being in him. The governesses had each one their own way of being in them. Each one had a certain effect on him.

It is very interesting that every one has in them their kind of stupid being. There is in every one their own way of living, of eating, of drinking, of beginning and ending, remembering and forgetting, of going on and stopping. Mr. Hersland was now in the beginning of his middle living. He was beginning then his habits of middle living. He had then in him eating and sleeping and hygiene and much beginning and hearty laughing and impatient being and a kind of interest in some people near him and some brushing away of his wife from around him and his regular derangements in his stomach and in his dieting. He had in him then the beginning of his middle living. Later in the ending of his middle living it came to be a more sodden repeating. Now repeating was in him a varied vigorous pounding.

There was then in Mr. Hersland in the beginning of his middle living beginning to be very completely in him as repeating his way of eating, of thinking, of laughing, of talking, of beginning, of having impatient feeling, of being attracted by women. There was then in him beginning accented repeating that later would be louder and have less changing in repeating. Now there is enough history of him. Now there will be a history of Mrs. Hersland and the important feeling she had in her with the third governess Madeleine Wyman.

Mrs. Hersland to herself was never cut off from rich right living. She was to herself cut off from Bridgepoint living, from eastern travelling, from southern feeling, she was not to herself cut off from rich living. She had done travelling when she was younger, travelling with a cousin and a sister, she was now to her feeling cut off from such living. Always then, eastern living, her early travelling, was a romance to her feeling, it was later a little a romance to her children. The three children later in their living had the feeling that Madeleine Wyman owned their mother's early Bridgepoint being, it gave to them a sore feeling. Not that Madeleine Wyman had any influence over any of them, over the mother or the father or any of the children. It was nothing of such a thing that happened to any of them. It was that she owned the mother of them by living in her feeling their mother's early living, by being the reason of their mother's having in her then when Madeleine Wyman was with them the being herself to herself more inside her in her being than at any other time in all her living.

Mrs. Hersland as I was saying was never important for her children excepting to begin them. She never had a feeling of herself to herself from them. She was of them until they were so big that she was lost among them, she was lost then between them and the father of them.

To begin again with Mr. Hersland and his choosing of the governess for the education of his children. To begin again with Mr. Hersland and his theories of education.

As I said the first governess was a real governess and knew french and german and was a good musician. Then his theories changed in him and he wanted a woman who was strong and used to farming and he got one and she was pleasanter for him for she had a physical meaning for him and then she married the baker and they all sometimes saw her after but that was the end of her governessing and for some time then they had no one. Then they heard of Madeleine Wyman who was everything. They needed a governess then so the father thought because the children had forgotten all their french and german and the daughter Martha that year had missed annual promotion. Besides in their country living they needed some one to keep the family living apart from the living around them. Anyway in Madeleine Wyman they had everything, she knew french and german, she was an american, she had had good american schooling, she was a fair musician, she was intelligent and could talk as well as listen to Mr. Hersland about education, she wanted to listen always to Mrs. Hersland's Bridgepoint living, she felt always the gentle fine being in Mrs. Hersland's country house living, she was good looking, she liked walking and wanted to learn swimming. She had everything, every one was content then, her parents were glad to have her in such a good situation, every one was suited then and then there was a beginning. Madeleine Wyman was the third governess the Herslands had living with them.

Madeleine Wyman's father and mother were both living. There were in all, four children. Madeleine was the oldest of them, then louise, then Frank, and then Helen. The Hersland children later knew all of them.

There are many ways then for women to like men, there are many ways for men to like women. Some women want a man to be florid and have a reddish beard when he has one, some want him brown with a black one, some then want health, some want youth in those near them. Many men and many women want those near them to have strongly in them the feeling and appearance of healthy being, many men say it of women and of trees and other things near them, that's a healthy looking one, that is in such of them the highest kind of commendation. Mr. Hersland was such a one. Not in the woman he needed for a wife for him, she was pretty and dark, and healthy enough looking but that was not in her a striking thing. Mr. Hersland wanted his children to be healthy looking, in choosing the second governess he chose her for this being in her. In his middle living he needed this kind of fine healthiness in women to content him, later he needed a more active being in them, they had then to be energetic enough around him to fill him in where he had been shrunk away then from the outside of him. In his middle living then he wanted a woman to have a good figure and to be healthy looking. The second governess had been such a one and Mr. Hersland always had a certain pleasure in having her in the house with them. Later when she had married the baker he sometimes on his way home would stop to eat a cake and talk to her, tell her about what was the best way to give milk to the baby, to keep strong and not to need a doctor, what kind of doctor she should have to take care of her, what was the right way for her to do to content her husband and save money and never have any trouble to come to her. He always gave advice to her; he ate a cake, he told her whether she was getting fatter or thinner, how to get thinner when she was getting fatter and later after she had had another baby and was always looking dragged and getting thinner, he would tell her what she should do to get fatter.

With Madeleine Wyman it was a different matter. She was healthy but not the kind to make one feel it in her. She had a trim figure, she was not pretty, nor ugly either, she was pleasant and bright and had some energy.

With her Mr. Hersland could always talk about education in a different way from that in which he talked with the second governess who had married the baker. Madeleine Wyman was young and had understanding in her, she was young and ready to try to carry out his theories in the way he wanted from her. He liked to talk to her but it was not a personal feeling. She had understanding in her, she was young and ready to carry out his feeling about education but really she was not very personal for him, she was very personal for Mrs. Hersland, she was to Mrs. Hersland a part of Mrs. Hersland's most important living.

Madeleine Wyman stayed with the Hersland's about three years and then there was a struggle for her by her family who wanted her to marry John Summer who wanted to marry her but was not very anxious to have her, and she had not about it any very strong feeling but she liked it with the Herslands as she was then living and she did not care very much about marrying. Later she married him and he was later then a more or less sick man with his own ways in him of eating and doctoring. He was a rich man and her family wanted she should marry him. She had no objection then, only she liked it so very well being with the Herslands then, she did not want any changing. There was no way really to convince her family that she was very well content to stay with the Herslands then, Mrs. Hersland tried to convince them. Once to convince them she paid double wages to Madeleine Wyman and had Madeleine a dress made then by Mary Maxworthing and Mabel Linker who made Mrs.

Hersland's dresses for visiting, to convince the Wyman family that Madeleine was best off with the Herslands then and should stay with them. There was then about three months of sharp struggle between the Wymans and Mrs. Hersland and Madeleine and a little Mr. Hersland with them. Then Madeleine had to leave them, the parents, that is the whole family of them, the Wyman family, would not listen to reason or to higher wages or even to a dress in the most fashionable way of dressmaking. John Summer was content to have Madeleine stay where she was then. Sometime he wanted to marry her but there was no hurry about it for him. Later Madeleine went home and later then she married him and later then they adopted a little girl, they could not have any children, and later then they gave up this one, and later then he took to ways of eating and ways of doctoring and then he was no longer working and they were rich enough then to try every kind of way of eating and travelling and doctoring and she was faithful to him and he died then and this was many years after and Mrs. Hersland and Mr. Hersland had been long dead then, but Mrs. Wyman was still living.

This is now as remembering the Wyman family and reconstructing the children from remembered parts of them and reconstructing the parents from the reconstructed children, this is what the Wyman family was then. This is now a history of them. They were, none of them, people to make a strong impression.

The mother and the father, Mr. and Mrs. Wyman were not so old then as they seemed to be to every one who knew them then. They were very foreign, that made them then with grown up children a very old man and a very old woman. They were not so very old then for they lived a long time after, longer than Mr. and Mrs. Hersland who were young then to them. Mr. Wyman then had a nature in him a dependent independent earthy instrument nature in him and all being was vague in him, Mrs. Wyman had independent dependent being and it was concentrated being but not very efficient being, it was enough to make some attacking in her being, it was enough to make such attacking pretty persistent and sometimes insinuating, rarely winning but very often annoying. She could be persistent, insinuating, and annoying.

The youngest daughter Helen was all spread and all vague in her nature. She had a good education for she was interested in studying, she was almost interested in writing. She was not so much interested in teaching but teaching was to be her occupation. There was no opening then for a girl like Helen except teaching, as I was saying she was almost interested in writing but this was never active enough inside her to start her going, just active enough inside her to make her more modern than her sister Madeleine who was the other one in the family who had had education. So then Helen was all spread and all vague in her independent dependent nature, but people who knew her had a friendly feeling for her. As I was saying she came almost to the point of being interested in writing but it remained as vague and spread out as her being, it never came to any thing. Later there was marrying in her living and that was a very strange proceeding.

The second daughter Louise was almost as concentrated as her mother but there was less to her nature. It came to about the same thing as efficient being, it made her less interesting, less menacing, more agreeable to be knowing. The important things in her living were the marrying, first of Madeleine, later the strange marrying of Helen and then the taking charge of her, later the helping her brother in his business of nurseryman; the keeping everything going in the later Wyman living when old Mrs. Wyman's methods had no more efficiency for their living. And so she succeeded to her mother's living, she never was married, she never bore children, as I was saying she was of her mother's being but there was less to her nature, there was less variety in her when she was younger, when she was in her middle living, when she was older. To herself inside her she was not more part of her mother and father than were her sisters and her brother. If she had known it she would not have liked it inside her. It was the marrying of her sisters and the business of her brother that were important to her not the being and the living in her father and her mother.

The son Frank was almost as vague in his nature as his father. He was tall then and had a long head and thick hair and at that time he had mild humor in him. He could make jokes at children, give him time he could make jokes at girls and at women. He was not slow but he was not very decided inside him. The father was darker and drier and seemed to be quicker. Really they had about the same nature, the two of them, neither of them had an efficient nature. The son had an easier life because he had his sisters, and his wife, later. He always all through his living was tall and slow and pleasant and mildly joking and not lazy and not active either and there was always the appearance as if his women, Louise and Madeleine and his wife and Helen were holding him up so that he would keep on standing. His mother had never done this for him. While she was directing the family he had been drifting. He tried one way of earning a living and then another way and then nothing. It was not till later that he became a nurseryman with women around him to support him. So Frank had a pleasant enough life all his living and successful enough life in his living.

The three Hersland children then were having their regular public school living, they had then all the feeling of country children. They had too then every kind of fancy education anything that their father could think would be good for them. The third governess was really then only to keep them up in music practicing and a little in french and german, mostly then just to be in the house with them. Mr. Hersland was just then deciding that what the children needed was to be kept going and Madeleine Wyman had enough education in every direction to keep them going. She had it in her later to give a sore feeling to the Hersland children by to them owning the father and the mother. Earlier when she was a governess to them Martha sometimes had had a little feeling against her when Madeleine tried to carry out Mr. Hersland's theories of education. The Hersland children were not accustomed to having any one really try to be systematic in such realization, they were accustomed to have only the pleasant new beginnings of new ways of learning and of out of door living. Mr. Hersland's living just then was the beginning of the middle living in his great fortune, the beginning of a struggling to resist a beginning of an ending to his fortune. He took less and less interest in the children just then excepting when they came up against him. Madeleine was conscientious in trying to realize the ideas she knew he had in him. This as I was saying was to Martha and a little to young David, interfering. Later Madeleine had her own trouble in her and the children then went on with their living as was natural to them, having their regular public school living, having all the feeling of country children, having various kinds of fancy education and outdoor living, being of them the poor people near them.

Mrs. Hersland then had in her her time of being most herself to herself in her feeling. Her important being was then existing from Madeleine Wyman's living in her being, being in her early living, later needing protection against her parents' nagging, needing to be held against them by extra wages which Mrs. Hersland induced Mr. Hersland to give her and a dress made by Mary Maxworthing and Mabel Linker.

In Mr. Hersland, his early living was not, then in his middle living, in him, in his feeling. It was in him as part of him, it came out of him sometimes in talking, it was not in him then in his middle living nor in his later living, it was not in him then in his feeling. It was not important to him excepting as so much talking coming out of him.

In Mrs. Hersland then it was a different thing, her early living was a continuous living that was going on then and she was cut off from it, to her feeling. It is clear then that Mrs. Hersland had in her early living in her as something that was in her, in her middle living, as part of her feeling. To herself in her feeling she was never cut off from right rich living, really then she was not at all of such living, later when she met any of such of them she was cut off from them, to herself then it was not that she was cut off from right rich living, to herself then it was a little then that she was cut off from her family living and eastern travelling and visiting. It always had been all through her Gossols living, a little in her. It had not, before Madeleine was in the habit of listening to her, it had not been in her, a conscious feeling. Later then it was more consciously in her, it was really then not an important part of her being, it was really then an important part of her feeling herself inside her in her being. This came to her later, this came to her when she told it over and over to Madeleine Wyman who was living then the complete being of Mr. and Mrs. Hersland in their early living.

Neither Madeleine Wyman nor Mrs. Hersland had in them really efficient being. They both had in them some resisting fighting, some yielding winning. It showed in the two of them in very different fashion. Mrs. Hersland did not know it inside her but she wanted Madeleine in the house with her, she wanted to have from her important being of herself to herself inside her. This was then in those years in the middle of her middle living her important being in her talking, and her important feeling; her early living, her marrying and her eastern travelling, Madeleine Wyman was then the important part of her important feeling. Her children were then not living by her being, her husband was then not living by her being, Madeleine Wyman was living by her being, from Madeleine Mrs. Hersland had then all her active important being and this is interesting.

Slowly every one in continuous repeating, to their minutest variation, comes to be clearer to some one. Sometime there will be an ordered history of every one. More and more then it is wonderful in living the subtle variations coming clear into ordered recognition, coming to make every one a part of some kind of them, some kind of men and women. Repeating then is in every one, every one then comes sometime to be clearer to some one, sometime there will be then an orderly history of every one who ever was or is or will be living.

I am writing for myself and strangers. This is the only way that I can do it. Everyone is a real one to me, everybody is like some one else too to me. No one of them that I know can want to know it and so I write for myself and strangers.

Mostly everyone dislikes to hear it. I love it and I write it. Mostly no one knowing me can like it that I love it that every one is of a kind of men and women, that always I am looking and comparing and classifying of them, always I am seeing their repeating. More and more I love it of them, the being in them, the mixing in them, the repeating in them, the deciding the kind of them every one is who has human being.

This is now a history of Martha Hersland. This is now a history of Martha and of every one who came to be of her living.

Every one then is an individual human being. Every one then is like many others always living, there are many ways of thinking of everyone, this is now a description of all of them. Now I will tell all the meaning to me in repeating, the loving there is in me for repeating.

Always from the beginning there was to me all living as repeating. Loving repeating is always in children. Some children have loving repeating in little things and story-telling, some have it as a more bottom being. Slowly this comes out in them in all their children being, in their eating, playing, crying, and laughing. Loving repeating is then in a way earth feeling. This is very strong in many, in children and in old age being. This is very strong in many in all ways of humorous being, this is very strong in some from their beginning to their ending.

As I was saying all little children have in them mostly very much loving repeating being. As they grow into bigger children some have it more some have it less in them. Mostly when they are growing to be young men and women they have it not in them to have loving repeating being in them as a conscious feeling. Many men and many women never have it in them the conscious feeling of loving repeating. Many men and many women never have it in them until old age weakening is in them, a consciousness of repeating. Many have it in them all their living as a conscious feeling as a humorous way of being in them. Some have it in them, the consciousness of always repeating the whole of them as a serious obligation.

Some find it interesting to find inside them repeating in them of some one they have known or some relation to them coming out of them, some never have any such feeling in them, some have not any liking for such being in them. Some like to see such being in others around them but not in themselves inside them.

The relation of learning to being, of thinking to feeling, of realization to emotion, all these and many others are very complicated questions.

Always then from the beginning there was in me always increasing as a conscious feeling loving repeating being, learning to know repeating in every one, hearing the whole being of any one always repeating in that one every minute of their living. It is very clear to me and to my feeling, it is very slow in developing, it is very important to make it clear now in writing, it must be done now with a slow description. To begin again then with it in my feeling, to begin again then to tell of the meaning to me in all repeating, of the loving there is in me for repeating.

Sometime every one becomes a whole one to me. For many years this was just forming in me. For many years loving repeating was a bottom to me, I was never thinking then of the meaning of it in me, it had nothing then much to do with the learning, the talking, the thinking, nor the living then in me. There was for many years a learning and talking and questioning in me and not listening to repeating in every one around me. Then slowly loving repeating being came to be a conscious feeling in me. Slowly then every one sometime became a whole one to me.

In loving repeating being then to completed understanding there must always be a feeling for all changing, a feeling for living being that is always in repeating.

There are many that I know and always more and more I know it. They are all of them repeating and I hear it. Always I love it, sometimes I get a little tired of it, mostly I am always ready to do it, always I love it.

Sometimes some one for many years is baffling. The repeated hearing, seeing, feeling of repeating in them does not give to me then a history of the complete being in them. Slowly then sometime it comes to be clearer of them, I begin again with listening, I feel new shades in repeating, parts of repeating that I was neglecting hearing, seeing, feeling come to have a louder beating. Many times I begin and then begin again. Always I must not begin a deadened following, always their repeating must be a fresh feeling in my hearing, seeing, feeling. Always I must admit all changing. Often listening to them is irritating, often it is dulling, always then there must be in me new beginning, always there must be in me steadily alive inside me my loving repeating being.

Every one is sometime a puzzle to me. Every one is sometime a whole being to me. Every one is puzzling to me, some for some reason others for other reasons, always every one is puzzling, sometime every one becomes a whole one to me, mostly then they go on repeating clearly to me the whole of them, sometimes they commence again to be a puzzle to me, sometimes I lose the way of hearing clearly the repeating of the whole of them that always every one is always doing. Sometimes I know and hear and feel and see all the repeating in some one, all the repeating that is the whole of some one but it always comes as pieces to me, it is never there to make a whole one to me. Always then I listen and come back again and again to listen to every one. Always then I am thinking and feeling the repeating in every one.

Everybody is a real one to me, everybody is like some one else too to me. Every one is always repeating the whole of them. Each one slowly comes to be a whole one to me. Each one slowly comes to be a whole one in me.

Every one is themselves inside them, mostly every one reminds some one of some other one of some other ones, every one has it to say of some one some of many, he is like such a one I see it in him, she is like some one else I can tell it by remembering. Mostly every one is sometimes thinking that some one else is resembling the one at whom they are then looking. People disagreeing about ways of being resembling, people seeing different ways of making kinds in them often makes such irritation, sometimes exciting, sometimes confusing, sometimes to some one puzzling.

There are many ways then of knowing kinds in men and women, there are many ways then, there is a way of feeling them as kinds of them by ways of doing that come from education and tradition, kinds of them that come from the ways that make a nation, there are ways of seeing kinds of them by the kind of learning in them, tastes, beliefs, fondness for walking, working, doing nothing, there are ways of feeling kinds of them in color resemblances and gentleness in them, and courage, and ways of showing angry feeling, there are ways of knowing resemblances in them from occupation giving certain habits to them, there are ways of seeing kinds in them from their being always young, always old in them, bright all of some of them, dull all of some of them, moral all of some of them, immoral all of some of them, lazy all of some of them, very energetic always some of them, then there are samenesses in the looks of many of them that makes kinds of them to some and sometime some one will know all the ways there are for people to be resembling, some one sometime then will have a completed history of all of them.

Everybody then is mostly a real one to me, everybody is now like some one and like some other one and then again like some other one and each one sometimes is a whole one to me.

Now there will be a description of very young living in one. This one, and the one I am now beginning describing is Martha Hersland and this is a little story of the acting in her of her being in her very young living, this one was a very little one then and she was running and she was in the street and it was a muddy one and she had an umbrella that she was dragging and she was crying. "I will throw the umbrella in the mud," she was saying, she was very little then, she was just beginning her schooling, "I will throw the umbrella in the mud" she said and no one was near her and she was dragging the umbrella and bitterness possessed her, "I will throw the umbrella in the mud" she was saying and nobody heard her, the others had run ahead to get home and they had left her, "I will throw the umbrella in the mud," and there was desperate anger in her; "I have throwed the umbrella in the mud" burst from her, she had thrown the umbrella in the mud and that was the end of it all in her.

It is very hard telling from any incident in any one's living what kind of being they have in them. Martha Hersland had independent dependent being but this that I have just been telling might have been in the living of a little one having independent dependent being, might have been in the living of a little one having dependent independent being, might have been in the living of a little one having a mixture in its being. As I was saying no one knowing this as having been Martha's way of acting then when she a little one was filled full of angry feeling, with despairing feeling, with responsible feeling, with frightened feeling, no one then could be very certain of the kind of being Martha had in her.

I was telling of the living of the Hersland family in Gossols on a ten acre place and of people living in small houses near them and it was then that Martha Hersland was a child and was knowing children. She knew some children at the public school near them where she and her brothers had their american education, some children that were living then in the small houses near the ten acre place where the Hersland family were living then as I was telling and some other children who knew these children. And then she knew some children who sometimes came to see them, the Hersland children, who were the kind of children she naturally should have been knowing, from the kind of people Mr. and Mrs. Hersland should naturally be knowing, but these children were never important in her living.

She was then, as a child, as a young girl, almost until she was a young woman of the being of those living in small houses near them.

When she was a very little one sometimes she wanted not to be existing. This is a very common thing in mostly every one in the beginning of their living. It is very interesting the way anybody feels about dying, about not existing, about everything, about every one. As I was saying it is hard to know the kind of being in any one from just a description of some thoughts, some feelings, some actions in them for it is in their feeling of themselves inside them that the kind of being in them shows in them and that comes out of them slowly in their living, that comes out of them always as repeating, this is very very difficult to make any one understand from a description of them. This is now what I am always trying.

As I was saying many little ones have a feeling about not wanting any more to be living, some want to have been dead when they were little babies and not knowing anything, some want to be dead then so that every one will miss them, some want to prove themselves all noble by dying, some are just tired of struggling when they are little ones, there are such ones, and some of such of them have independent dependent being that does not succeed then in winning fighting by attacking.

To those knowing Martha Hersland then when she was a young one when she was beginning her individual being, she was then a whole one, to no one quite entirely pleasing, but most of those knowing her then liked her well enough whenever they thought about her and sometimes then they did not like her.

As I was saying then when she was a very little one and she was coming home with them, they went faster than she could then, they left her then and she was running with the umbrella one of them had left with her after saying she would carry it for her and she was saying I will throw the umbrella in the mud and then she was crying, I have thrown the umbrella in the mud, and then later she got home and the umbrella was not with her but one of the other ones one of those who had left her went back that day later and got it for her. Then she was a very little one and just beginning knowing the children near her. When she was a little bigger she was in her living almost entirely of them the people near her. As I was saying they mostly all liked her well enough when they thought about her, they did not think very much about her, sometimes when they thought about her they did not like her. She was for them mostly then as if she had been one of them in her natural way of living, there was nothing in her to make her a different kind of child from the others of them, she was of them and yet a little sometimes it was troublesome to her and for them in her that she was not of them in the living that would have been natural for her.

As I was saying Mr. Hersland had a strong feeling about educating his children. Sometimes when they were too much of one kind of living he had a new theory of independence for them that took the form of restrictions on the liberty they were enjoying and sometimes he wanted that they should be as they would have been if they had had the living that would have been natural for them and this came to him a few times in the living of his daughter Martha and he tried to make her over but mostly he wanted them to have an education making them to be strong and independent. About their living the life of the poor people near them, he never really thought about this in them. His feeling about his daughter Martha then in the beginning was that she was

119

of them, later that she could learn from them what they all knew in living, later when she sometimes met people it would have been natural she should be knowing he was impatient at the way she was looking and he was full up then with impatient feeling. Martha was hard-working and did well enough in her schooling but when he wanted her to have disciplining, to make strong beginnings in french and german and music and swimming and exercising and dancing, as I was saying she was always a little mixed up in beginning and then had a nervous confusion from the changing and Madeleine Wyman was thorough and annoying to her and then Martha was completely of them the poorer people near them.

So then Martha's young living was very confusing to her then but she did not know it in her then. All of her when it was in motion just was sort of knocking together, and that was mostly all the active being in her and that was to many who knew her obstinacy and resisting in her and to her father it was that she was never thorough. Sometimes there was a stronger reaction for a moment in her, anger, or a deep commotion for something that was a disgrace to some one or to her and then she was a little more than the whole one that she mostly just was and was mostly to every one.

This was then the being in her. When she was quite a young one, as I was saying, she was then quite completely of the living of the children and the people living near the Hersland family then when the Hersland family were living in that part of Gossols where no other rich people were living then. She could have happen to her then what could happen to any of them in their living, in their schooling, in their playing, in their quarrelling, in their liking, in their disliking, in their being interesting one to the other of them.

As I was saying Martha Hersland was not then very interesting to any of them, she was good enough at doing anything, they were friends enough with her most of them, they did not most of them think very well of the way she did quarrelling whenever she did any of that with any of them. One little boy wanted her to do loving the little boy who with his sister lived with the father who smoked to help his asthma but this was not very much of a success for Martha then had a nervous feeling and was not very daring and was not very understanding and had a confusion that was a little like wanting, a little like obstinate hesitation, a little like being afraid of everything, a little like a very stupid way of being, and the little boy then forgot about her being existing for really Martha was not then to any one very interesting.

When she was a little older she was still always with them the people near the Hersland family then in that part of Gossols where no rich people were living then. She was with them then living their kind of being, hearing them talking and knowing everything happening to them but not any of them then included her with them in quarrelling or loving, not even as making a beginning. The natural future for her was then separating them. She was still very much with them, with the girls she would help the mothers cooking or setting the table, she knew their daily living, she helped them in wiping the dishes when they were washing them, and she was with them and always then she was not of them even as she had been to them when she was a younger one and she never knew it then and they never knew it then.

No one knew very much what Martha was feeling about anything when she was in her young living. She was not ever telling very much of her feeling then to any one, and never to any one in the family living. Not any of the Hersland family ever were telling each other very much about what feeling they had in them. Martha was really not telling any one very much in her young living the feeling she had in her about anything and then in a way too it was not in her ready for telling.

I was saying that there was one family living in a small house near the Hersland family then of a mother a foreign woman who was rather wooden, and a father who was not important to any one, and three daughters who each one sometime came to have real beauty in them. It was the second one of them whom Martha knew very well in the later part of her young living. She had not come yet to have beauty in her this one, she was just beginning to work out to learn dress-making. The older one who was working in the city somewhere had come to have her beauty and there were queer things one heard then about her of her marrying a rich man, a man whose family made much money making chocolate and every one had heard of them from eating the chocolate they were making and the name sounded very italian and somehow every one knew though no one of them had ever seen him that he was a handsome fierce looking black-moustached man and a very rich one. None of the family of this girl ever said anything, Martha Hersland did not know really where she heard all about the oldest girl for when she thought it over she knew no one had told her. She knew dimly that all of them the three Banks boys one of whom was learning telegraphing, one of whom was learning shoemaking, the other learning nothing and perhaps sometimes stealing something, she knew they knew the three girls and said things to them that Martha was never really hearing but as I was saying Martha was not really interesting then to any one and inside, her feeling was not active to be to herself or to any one a thing possibly having then any expression. The young Rodman boy was to her a little more an active awakening because he said things to make her be understanding. There were two of them, the eldest a big lumbering fellow and this young one who made fun of her whenever he saw her and he just annoyed her and that was not really very active then in her.

Some of them, the younger ones whom she knew then were beginning to go out working and she saw them when they came back from their working and she was with them then and she was with them then again in the evening. Sometimes Mr. Hersland suddenly remembered that Martha should not go out in the evening, mostly he did not pay much attention to the daily feeling and the daily living in her then. Sometimes as I was saying he would suddenly remember she should not go out in the evening alone with these young people near them and then he would forbid her going and he would tell her that she should stay in the house and be with her mother and then he would lecture her brother that he did not take better care of his sister. "You have to take care of her sometime and you might as well begin, the sooner the better. You will have to do it sooner or later, I tell you." "I'll take mine later" said the brother but he was careful that his father did not hear and he went out that evening as he did many evenings as I will be telling later in the long history of the living of him, but on that evening Martha Hersland could not go out to be with the others.

As I was saying she was then not really very interesting to any one. She might have been a little interesting a couple of evenings to Harry Brenner but she never really was interesting to him.

As I was saying she was not so interesting to any of them as they were to each other then and she was not feeling and living and understanding anything really in the way they were doing then. As I was saying she almost might have been interesting to them from her almost being interesting a couple of evenings to Harry Brenner who was one of them but she did not come to be really interesting to him.

No one knew anything very much then of what she was feeling about anything then and she did not know what she felt then about anything in living and nobody knew what she felt then about living and really she did not clearly then feel anything.

This was the way she was then when one day when she was alone in another part of town where she had gone to take a lesson in singing she saw a man hit a woman with an umbrella, and the woman had a red face partly in anger and partly in asking and the man wanted the woman to know then that he wanted her to leave him alone then in a public street where people were passing and Martha saw this and this man was for her the ending of the living I have been describing that she had been living. She would go to college, she knew it then and understand everything and know the meaning of the living and the feeling in men and in women. This is to be now more history of, in her, the ending of her older young living and her subsequent going to college and of the man she met there and who there married her.

In the description of her that I have been writing so far Martha has been a very little one, a baby, and then a little one and then a young girl and then about to become a young woman and always then in a way to herself inside her and to every one knowing her she had been the same whole one.

This was then as I was saying in a way always true she was always the same whole one inside her and to every one ever knowing her.

As I was saying she started then her preparation to get for herself a college education. Her father Mr. Hersland was not very much interested just then in his children. She had teachers and she could be taught enough by them to pass her entrance examination. She began a little then to know other kinds of young girls and boys than those that she had until then been knowing. She played duets in the evening and sang with John Davidson who was preparing to go away to get an eastern education.

She was less and less and then almost not at all with them the people living near the Hersland family then, and then as I was saying she went to get her college education.

As I was saying there was not then very much change in the being of her, she was always then the same whole one, at first there was a little more movement in her, she learned a little at first how to have definite feeling in her, she learned that in the college life around her but it was not really the being in her and all this will come out in the history of her. Martha went away to college then, as I was saying, and there she was learning to be like them the young men and women of her generation and there as I was saying she came to know Phillip Redfern.

Philip Redfern was born in a small city and in the south western part of this country. He was the son of a consciously ill-assorted pair of parents and his earliest intellectual concept so in his later living he was always saying, was the realization of the quality of these two decisive and unharmonized elements in his child life.

His mother was his dear dear friend then and from her he received then all the thoughts and convictions that were definite and conscious then and for a long time after in him. She was an eager, impetuous, sensitive creature, full of ideal enthusiasms in her being, with moments of clear purpose and vigorous thinking but for the most part was excitably prejudiced and inconsequent in sensitive enthusiasm and given to accepting and giving and living sensations and impressions under the conviction that she had them as carefully thought out theories and principles that were complete from reasoning. Her constant rebellion against the pressure of her husband's steady domination found effective expression in the inspiring training of her son to be the champion of women. It would be a sublime proof of the justice of all the poetry of living so she was always thinking for the son of James Redfern to devote the strength of the father that was soon to be in the son of him to the winning of liberty, equality, opportunity, beauty, feeling, for all women.

James Redfern was a man determined to be master always in his own house. He was a man courteous and deferential to all women, he never came into any vivid relation with any human being. He was cold and reserved and had a strong calm attacking will in him, and he was always perfectly right in doing everything. This was always true of him. He never knew it in him that his wife had a set purpose in her to make their son any particular thing in living. Such a thing could never be a real thing to him, such a thing no woman he could have living in the house with him could have in her, to him. It would not have any meaning excepting as words if she had ever said it to him. The things that have no meaning as existing are to every one very many, and that is always more and more important in understanding the being in men and women. Often it is very astonishing, it is like seeing something and some one who always has been walking with you and you always have been feeling that one was seeing everything with you and you feel then that they are seeing that thing the way you are seeing it then and you go sometime with that one to a doctor to have that one have their eyes examined and then you find that things you are seeing they cannot see and never have been seeing and it is very astonishing and everything is different and you know then that you are seeing, you are writing completely only for one and that one is yourself then and to every other one it is a different thing and then you remember every one has said that sometime and you know it then and it is astonishing.

Phillip Redfern when he was a man was to most every one who ever came to know him a person having in him a strange and incalculable nature. The strong enthusiasm of emotion of his mother's nature early awoke in him with the stimulation she was always then giving to him very much interest to him for the emotional life he could have in him. The interest for knowledge and domination were in him equally strong and from the beginning he devoted himself to meditation and analysis of the emotions he had in him. The constant spectacle of an armed neutrality between his parents early filled him with an interest in the nature of marriage and the meaning of women.

The college of which Redfern became a member was the typical co-educational college of the west, a completely democratic institution. Mostly no one there was conscious of a grand-father unless as remembering one as an old man living in the house with them or as living in another place and being written to sometimes by them and then having died and that was the end of grand-fathers to them. No one was really interested how any man or woman of them came by the money that was educating them, whether it came through several generations of gentlemen to them, whether it came through two generations or one, whether one of them earned it for herself or for himself by working, or teaching, or working on a farm or at book-selling or at anything else that would bring money to them in the summer or whether they earned a little by being a janitor to a school building in the winter or had it given them by someone interested in them. This democracy was then almost complete among them and was the same between the men and women as between the men, as between the women. The students were many of them earnest experienced men and women who had already struggled solidly with poverty and education. Many of them were interested in the sciences and the practical application of them but also there was among them a kind of feeling and yearning for beauty and this then often showed itself in them in much out of door wandering, and was beginning a little with some of them to realize itself in attempting making pictures and sculpture.

Among the many vigorous young women in the place there was Martha Hersland. She was a blond good-looking young woman full of moral purpose and educational desires. She had an eager earnest intelligence, fixed convictions and principles by then, and restless energy. She and Redfern were students in the same studies in the same class and soon singled themselves out from the crowd, it was all new, strange and dangerous for the south-western man and all perfectly simple and matter of course for the western girl. They spent much time in explaining to each other what neither quite understood. He never quite felt the reality of her simple convictions, she never quite realized what it was he did not understand.

One spring day a boy friend came to see her a younger brother of John Davidson who used to play duets with her and all three went out in the country. It was a soft warm day, the ground was warm and wet and they were healthy and they did not mind that. They found a fairly dry hill-side and sat down all three too indolent to wander further. The young fellow, a boy of eighteen, threw himself on the ground and rested his head on Martha Hersland's lap. Redfern did not stop a start of surprise and Martha Hersland smiled. The next day Redfern frankly came to her with his perplexity. "I don't understand," he said. "Was it alright for Davidson to do so yesterday. I almost believed it was my duty to knock him off." "Yes I saw you were surprised," she said and she looked uneasy and then she resolutely tried to make him see. "Do you know that to me a western woman it seems very strange that any one should see any wrong in this action. Yes I will say it, I have never understood before why you always seemed on guard." She ended pretty steadily, he flushed and looked uneasy.

After two years of marriage Redfern's realization of her was almost complete. Martha was all that she had promised him to be, all that he had thought her, but that all proved sufficiently inadequate to his needs. He knew she must suffer but what could he do. They were man and wife, their minds and natures were separated by great gulfs, it must be again an armed neutrality but this time it was not as with his parents an armed neutrality between equals but with an inferior who could not learn the rules of the game. It was just so much the more unhappy.

Mrs. Redfern never understood what had happened to her. In a dazed blind way she tried all ways of breaking through the walls that confined her. She threw herself against them with impatient energy and again she tried to destroy them piece by piece. She was always thrown back bruised and dazed and never quite certain whence came the blow, how it was dealt or why. It was a long agony, she never became wiser or more indifferent, she struggled on always in the same dazed eager way.

Such was the relation between Redfern and his wife when Redfern having made some reputation for himself in philosophy was called to Farnham college to fill the chair of philosophy there.

There was then a dean presiding over the college of Farnham who in common with many of her generation believed wholly in the essential sameness of sex and who had devoted her life to the development of this doctrine. The Dean of Farnham had had great influence in the lives of many women. She was possessed of a strong purpose and vast energy. She had an extraordinary instinct for the qualities of men and rarely failed to choose the best of the young teachers as they came from the universities. She rarely kept them many years for either they attained such distinction that the great universities claimed them or they were dismissed as not being able enough to be called away.

The new professor of philosophy was invited by the dean to meet the assembled faculty at a tea at her house two days after his arrival in the place. He entered alone and was met by the dean who was then just about beginning the ending of her middle living. She was a dignified figure with a noble head and a preoccupied abrupt manner. She was a member of a family which was proud of having had in three successive generations three remarkable women.

The first of these three was not known beyond her own community among whom she had great influence by reason of her strength of will, her powerful intellect, her strong common sense and her deep religious feeling. She carried to its utmost the then woman's life with its keen worldly sense, its power of emotion and prayer and its devout practical morality.

The daughter of this vigorous woman was known to a wider circle and sought for truth in all varieties of ecstatic experience. She mingled with her genuine mystic exaltation a basal common sense and though spending the greater part of her life in examining and actively taking part in all the exaggerated religious enthusiasms of her time she never lost her sense of criticism and judgement and though convinced again and again of the folly and hypocrisy of successive saints never doubted the validity of mystic religious experience.

In the third generation the niece of this woman, the dean Hannah Charles, found her expression in still wider experience. She did not expect her regeneration from religious experience and found her exaltation in resisting.

Through her influence she was enabled to keep the college in a flourishing state and to keep the control of all things entirely in her own hands but she was anxious that in the teaching staff there should be someone who would be permanent, who would have great parts and a scholarly mind and would have no influence to trouble hers and before many years she found Miss Dounor who ideally fulfilled these conditions.

Miss Dounor was a graduate of an eastern college and had made some reputation. She was utterly unattached, being an only child whose parents died just before she entered college and was equally detached by her nature from all affairs of the world and was always quite content to remain where she was so long as some took from her all management of practical affairs and left her in peace with her work and her dreams. She was possessed of a sort of transfigured innocence which made a deep impression on the vigorous practical mind of Miss Charles who while keeping her completely under her control was nevertheless in awe of her blindness of worldly things and of the intellectual power of her clear sensitive mind.

Though Miss Dounor was detached by the quality of her nature from worldly affairs it was not because she loved best dreams and abstract thought, for her deepest interest was in the varieties of human experience and her constant desire was to partake of all human relations but by some quality of her nature she never succeeded in really touching any human creature she knew. Her transfigured innocence, too, was not an ignorance of the facts of life nor a puritan's instinct indeed her desire was to experience the extreme forms of sensuous life and to make even immoral experiences her own. Her detachment was due to an abstracted spirit that could not do what it would and which was evident in her reserved body, her shy eyes and gentle face.

As I was saying Phillip Redfern had been invited by the dean to meet the assembled faculty at a tea at her house. He entered in some wonder of anticipation and excitement of mind and was met by the dean Miss Charles, "You must meet Miss Dounor" she said to him breaking abruptly through the politeness of the new instructor who was as I said south-western. Redfern looked with interest at this new presentment of gentleness and intelligence who greeted him with awkward shyness. Her talk was serious pleasant and intense, her point of view clear, her arguments just, and her opinions sensitive. Her self-consciousness disappeared during this eager discussion but her manner did not lose its awkward restraint, her voice its gentleness or her eyes their shyness.

While the two were still in the height of the discussion there came up to them a blond, eager, good-looking young woman whom Redfern observing presented as his wife to his new acquaintance. Miss Dounor checked in her talk was thrown into even more than her original shy awkwardness and looking with distress at this new arrival after several efforts to bring her mind to understand said, "Mrs. Redfern yes yes, of course, your wife I had forgotten." She made another attempt to begin to speak and then suddenly giving it up gazed at them quite helpless.

"Pray go on as I am very anxious to hear what you think," said Mrs. Redfern nervously and Redfern bowing to his wife turned again to Miss Dounor and went on with the talk.

An observer would have found it difficult to tell from the mere appearance of these three what their relation toward each other was. Miss Dounor was absorbed in her talk and thought and oblivious of everything except the discussion, her shy eyes fixed on Redfern's face and her tall constrained body filled with eagerness, Redfern was listening and answering showing the same degree of courteous deference to both his companions, turned first toward one and then toward the other one with impartial attention and Mrs. Redfern her blond good-looking face filled with eager anxiety to understand listened to one and then the other with the same anxious care.

Later Redfern wandered to a window where Miss Hannah Charles, Miss Dounor and Mrs. Redfern were standing looking out at a fine prospect of sunset and a long line of elms defining a road that led back through the town of Farnham to the wooded hills behind. Mrs. Redfern was listening intently to each one's thinking. "Ah of course you know Greek," she said with eager admiration to Miss Dounor who made no reply.

It is the french habit in thinking to consider that in the grouping of two and an extra it is the two that get something from it all who are of importance and whose

135

claim should be considered; the american mind accustomed to waste happiness and be reckless of joy finds morality more important than ecstacy and the lonely extra of more value than the happy two. To our new world feeling the sadness of pain has more dignity than the beauty of joy. It takes time to learn the value of happiness.

Martha Redfern eager, anxious and moral had little understanding of the sanctity of joy and hardly a realization of the misery of pain. She understood little now what it was that had come upon her and she tried to arrange and explain it by her western morality and her new world humanity. She could not escape the knowledge that something stronger than community of interest bound her husband and Miss Dounor together. She tried resolutely to interpret it all in terms of comradeship and great equality of intellectual interests never admitting to herself for a moment the conception of a possible marital disloyalty. But in spite of these standards and convictions she was filled with a vague uneasiness that had a different meaning than the habitual struggle against the hard wall of courtesy that Redfern had erected before her.

This struggle in her mind showed itself clearly when she was in the company of her husband and Miss Dounor. She would sit conscientiously bending her mind to her self-imposed task of understanding and development, when in the immediate circle of talkers that included her husband and Miss Dounor she gave anxious and impartial attention to the words of one and the other occasionally joining in the talk by an earnest inquiry and receiving always from Redfern the courteous deference that he extended to every one, to everything, to all women. She listened with admiring attention particularly to Miss Dounor who genuinely unconscious of all this nervous misery paid her in return scant attention.

One afternoon in the late fall of the second year of their life at Farnham, Miss Charles came to the room where she was sitting alone and in her abrupt way spoke directly to the object of her visit. She stopped and looked steadily at the uneasy woman who was dazed by this sudden statement of her own suspicion, "I, I don't understand," she stammered. "I think you understand quite well. I depend upon you to speak to him about it," and with this the dean departed.

Categories that once to some one had real meaning can later to that some one be all empty. It is queer that words that meant something in our thinking and our feeling can later come to have in them in us not at all any meaning. This is happening very often to almost every one having any realization in them in their feeling, in their thinking, in their imagining of the words they are always using.

This is very true then, this is very true then of the feeling and the thinking that makes the meaning in the words one is using, this is very true then that to many of them having in them strongly a sense of realizing the meaning of the words they are using that some words they once were using, later have not any meaning and some then have a little shame in them when they are copying an old piece of writing where they were using words that sometime had real meaning for them and now have not any real meaning in them to the feeling and the thinking and the imagining of such a one. Often this is in me in my feeling, often then I have to lose words I have once been using, now I commence again with words that have meaning, a little perhaps I had forgotten when it came to copying the meaning in some of the words I have just been writing. Now to begin again with what I know of the being in Phillip Redfern, now to begin again a description of Phillip Redfern and always now I will be using words having in my feeling, thinking, imagining very real meaning.

He was of the kind of men and women who, in the end, to every one, have been as if they had been a failure. These see themselves, always have, do and will see themselves all their living as virtuous, as heroic, as noble, as successful, as beautiful, as whatever is the best way of being to them, see themselves so through the weakness as well as through the strong things in them.

Johnson when he forgets his emotion, the emotion he had when he was friendly or loving or fighting, Johnson when he forgets his emotion and declares it to have been all the other one's doing attributes his having yielded to this indulging in loving, fighting, friendly action, to the weakness in him of always yielding. Frank Hackart attributes his doing anything to the philanthropy in him, she was lonesome and threw herself on him, took possession and what did he do but take care of her. Mary Helbing always puts it down to, that they wanted it and she gave it but she had no responsibility, it was because she was so game that she did it, that is always the reason she does it, she is so game she never refuses anything that is a challenge, there is never anything that she is ever wanting in her living that she is ever getting. Sarah Sands puts her yielding down to unsuspiciousness, that is the reason she yields, she is so easy, that is the secret of it. Phillip Redfern was of this kind of them, he was to himself completely chivalrous, completely a gentleman, women, every one should always have complete courtesy always from him. And they are right all of them, all these things, each thing in each one, are characteristics in each one but they all think that one characteristic is the whole of them, they all of them forget the other things in them that are active in them, they all have it in common that in remembering anything they forget all the emotion they had then in them and so it must have been the other person's fault it happened, anything.

As I was saying Phillip Redfern was of the kind of men and women, and there are always many men of this kind of them and some women of this kind of them, who have in their living a good deal of reputation from the living and the being in them and then they are not successful in living successful in the whole of their living and to many knowing them they are romantic in their living, or beautiful, or dramatic in their living and to some, saints in living, and Redfern was such a one and to most every one he was a man always failing in his living, and to Miss Dounor he was a saint among men and to Mrs. Redfern he was wonderful in the honorable courtesy in him and mostly every one sometime thought he was a bad man and mostly to every one he was a man given to lying. He said once of some one, "Lathrop tells a lie as if it were the truth and I tell the truth as if it were a lie." He was to himself a man simple, sensuous and passionate and that was to himself the whole of him.

For the rest of his days he was a literary man and sometimes a politician. He plunged deeply into the political life of his time and failed everywhere, in this life as in all of his human relations his instincts gave the lie to his ideals and his ideals to his instincts.

Phillip Redfern was to Miss Dounor a man of saintly strength and courage and chivalrous feeling and self-sacrificing. Phillip Redfern was to Mrs. Redfern a man before whom she wanted to be intelligent, and honorable in acting and in feeling and delicate, and to be pleasing by knowing Greek and naive realism. Phillip Redfern was to very many a man who was always lying. Phillip Redfern was to very many a man always wronging every one.

Mostly every one has some way of finding themselves inside them more or less distinguished, they have this feeling mostly every one, more or less inside them always in their living. Being virtuous, being sentimental, being dramatic, being religious, being anything is interesting in each one having in them that thing that they have in them. Being distinguished each one inside them by something, to themselves in their feeling, is very interesting. All these things are to me very interesting.

Perhaps no one will ever know the complete history of every one. This is a sad thing. Perhaps no one will ever have as a complete thing the history of any one. Surely some one sometime will have a complete history of some one. All this gives to some a very despairing feeling. Some one is hearing something, and they think then, it is only by an accident that I have heard that thing, I have known that thing, always there are many things that I am not knowing, that is very certain, every one always is repeating, that there is not any denying, certainly sometime some one always paying all attention must know sometime the history of some one.

It is a very difficult thing to know it of any one whether they are enjoying anything, whether they are knowing they are giving pain to some one, whether they were planning that thing. It is hard to know such things in any one when they are telling when they are not telling to any one what they know inside them. It is hard telling it of any one whether they are enjoying a thing, whether they know that they are hurting some one, whether they have been planning the acting they have been doing. It is hard to know it if they tell you all they know of it.

Miss Cora Dounor could do some planning, could do some attacking with it, that is certain. This is perhaps surprising to some reading.

Miss Dounor held Miss Charles from really touching her real being, she did not hold her from really touching Redfern's being. She never recognized this failing in herself inside her but it was a failing of the completeness of pride in her and later much later when Redfern was no longer existing in living it made them separate from one another, later it in spots made Miss Dounor bitter. Miss Charles then was not succeeding in keeping Miss Dounor with her, she was winning by not then having any remembrance in her of the trouble she had had in her.

Miss Charles was of the kind of them the kind in men and women I know very well in living. I know very well all the varieties of this kind. Miss Charles was of a kind of men and women I know very well in all the kind of ways of being they have in them. She was as I was saying in her younger living aggressive in her detailed and generalized conviction of morality and reformation and equalization. Being nice or not a nice kind of one, a pleasant or unpleasant kind of one was not in her an important thing. Later in her living she went on in the direction she had been going but her methods then were from the being in her and that then mostly entirely filled her. That made her control everything, every one near her by steady resisting pressure and that was then the way of winning in her. Everything near her, every one near her, every detail of everything was then more or less completely owned by her. Later as I was saying Miss Dounor left her, Miss Charles had a little owned Redfern almost and Miss Dounor many years later left her and Miss Charles went on always to her ending completely owning the college of Farnham.

The Redferns after the ending of their living at the college of Farnham never lived anywhere together again. Mrs. Redfern never understood this thing. Always she was expecting it to begin again, their living together and always she was studying and preparing herself to be a companion to him in intellectual living. Always then she was studying and striving and travelling and working. And then he was dead and then she knew they would not live together again. Then she was certain of this thing.

That was her living then until he was dead and she went back to the ten acre place where then her father and mother were living and her mother was weakening then and a little while later then she died there and Martha finished her living staying with her father who had then lost his great fortune.

No one knowing Mr. Hersland in his middle living could have really been completely certain that he would never bring through to a completed beginning anything in his living. Later in the ending of his middle living he was beginning to lose his great fortune. His wife was dying and dead then and Martha was living with him and his sons Alfred and David were in Bridgepoint then. He was full up then pretty nearly with impatient feeling. Martha had no understanding in desiring, she would always after a meal offer him sugar to put in his coffee and he never took sugar in black coffee and she never learned this thing and he was then completely filled up with impatient feeling. He never liked to be helped in putting on anything and always Martha helped him on with his coat and always he would be completely then filled up with impatient feeling.

No one knowing Mr. Hersland in his middle living could have really been completely certain that he would never bring through to a completed beginning anything in his living. No one knowing Mr. Hersland up to the ending of his middle living, not any of the men knowing him, feeling him, seeing him, hearing him, hearing about him, working with him, working against, working with him some and against him some, not any man or any woman or any of his children could really be certain about him before the ending of his middle living, from any way of knowing, from knowing anything about him or in him could really be certain that he would not be succeeding in living.

He was then beginning definitely not succeeding in living, he was beginning then really losing his great fortune.

It is so very exceedingly a difficult thing to know about the going to be succeeding, the going to be failing in living in a very great many men and women, it is an exceedingly difficult thing although one can know of them all the being they have in them, all the variations of repeating of the being in them ever coming out of them. It is an exceedingly difficult thing in very many women and in very many men to know it of them whether they will be succeeding or failing in living. It is an exceedingly difficult thing to know it of any one.

I have been giving the history of a very great many men and women. Sometime I will give a history of every kind of men and women, every kind there is of men and women. Already I have given a history of many men and women. Sometime I will be giving a history of all the rest of them. This is now pretty nearly certain.

Sometime I want to understand every kind of way any one can have the feeling of being distinguished by the virtue they have in them. Being distinguished each one inside them by something, to themselves in their feeling, is very interesting. Being right each one inside them by something to themselves in their feeling is very interesting.

Many have a certain feeling a sure feeling, about something inside them. Many need company for it, this is very very common. Many need a measure for it, this will need explaining. Some need drama to support it, some need lying to help it, some love it, some hate it, some never are very certain they really have it.

Some out of their own virtue make a god who sometimes later is a terror to them. Some make some things like laws out of the nature of them, out of the nature of some other one. Some are controlled by other people's virtue, and then it scares them. Listen to each one telling about their own virtue and that grows to make a god for them, grows to be a law for them and often afterward scares them, some afterwards like it, some forget it, some are it.

I want to know sometime all about sentimental feeling. I want to know sometime all the different kinds of ways people have it in them to be certain of anything. Always more and more I want to know it of each one what certainty means to them, how they come to be certain of anything, what certainty means to them and how contradiction does not worry them and how it does worry them and how much they have in them of remembering and how much they have in them of forgetting, and how different any one is from any other one and what any one and every one means by anything they are saying.

Some have certainty by comparison, by comparing the thing they have then with what any other one they are knowing, hearing, seeing is having, some never compare anything with anything in any one, certainty is a real thing in some, in some of such of them as a little pile they are gradually increasing, in some as something that they keep there inside them always of the same dimension, in some as something they have because they are defending that thing, in some as something they have because they are attacking some one for that thing, in some as something that gives to them for that thing a stubborn feeling in them. Some have it and lose it while they are speaking. Quite a number have it and lose it while they are speaking or acting. Some are very energetic to express it but always they do not have it in them. Some need company to keep any certainty in them, some like company around them while they have their own certainty inside them, some need to have the certainty in the presence of the company that they need to have with them always in their living. Certainty and virtuous feeling and important feeling in men and women is very interesting.

It makes me a little unhappy that everything is a little funny. It makes me a little unhappy that every one seems sometime almost a little crazy. It does make me sometime a little uncertain, it does sometime make me very uncertain about everything and always then it is perplexing what is certain what is not certain, who is a queer one, what is a funny thing for some one to be wanting or not wanting or doing or not doing or thinking or not thinking or believing or not believing.

As I have been saying each one has their own being in them, each one has their own sensitiveness to things in them, each one is of a kind of them.

Disillusionment in living is finding that no one can really ever be agreeing with you completely in anything. This is the real thing of disillusion that no one, not any one really is believing, seeing, understanding, thinking anything as you are thinking, believing, seeing, understanding such a thing. This is then the real meaning of not being any longer a young one in living, the complete realizing that not any one really can believe what any other one is believing and some there are, enough of them, who never have completely such a realization, they are always hoping to find her or him, they are always changing her or him to fit them, they are always looking, they are always forgetting failing or explaining it by something, they are always going on and on in trying.

Young ones sometimes think they have it in them, this thing, some young ones kill themselves then, stop living then, this is often happening, young ones sometimes very often even, think they have in them this thing but they do not have it in them, mostly not any young one, as a complete realization, this thing, they have it in them and it is sometimes, very often then an agony to them, some of them kill themselves or are killed then, but really mostly not any of them have realized the thing, they may be dead from this thing, they have not realized the thing.

Disillusionment in living is the finding that nobody agrees with you not those that are fighting for you. Complete disillusionment is when you realize that no one can for they can't change. The amount they agree with you is important to you until the amount they do not agree with you is completely realized by you. Then you say you will write for yourself and strangers, you will be for yourself and strangers and this then makes an old man or an old woman of you.

This is then one thing, another thing is the perfect joy of finding some one, any one really liking something you are liking, making, doing, being. This is another thing and a very pleasant thing, sometimes not a pleasant thing at all. That depends on many things, on some thing.

It is a very strange feeling when one is loving a clock that is to every one of your class of living an ugly and a foolish one and one really likes such a thing and likes it very much and liking it is a serious thing, or one likes a colored handkerchief that is very gay and every one of your kind of living thinks it a very ugly or a foolish thing and thinks you like it because it is a funny thing to like it and you like it with a serious feeling, or you like eating something and liking it is a childish thing to every one or you like something that is a dirty thing and no one can really like that thing or you write a book and while you write it you are ashamed for every one must think you are a silly one or a crazy one and yet you write it and you are ashamed, you know you will be laughed at or pitied by every one and you have a queer feeling and you are not very certain and you go on writing. Then some one says yes to it, to something you are liking, or doing or making and then never again can you have completely such a feeling of being afraid and ashamed that you had then when you were writing or liking the thing and not any one had said yes about the thing. In a way it is a very difficult thing to like anything, to do anything.

As I was saying in many there is the slow reacting, slow expressing being that comes more and more in their living to determine them. There are in many of such ones aspirations and convictions due to quick reactions to others around them, to books they are reading, to the family tradition, to the spirit of the age in educating, in believing, to the lack of power of articulating the being in them that makes them need then to be filled full with other reactions in them so that they will then have something. Some of such of them spend all their living in adjusting the being that comes to active condition inside them in their living to the being that they have come to be in living from all being that has been affecting them in all their living, some of such of them want a little in them to create their living from the being inside them and they have not the power in them for this thing, they go on then living the being of every one that has been making them. It is a wonderful thing as I was saying and am now repeating, it is a wonderful thing how much a thing needs to be in one as a desire in them how much courage any one must have in them to be doing anything if they are a first one, if it is something no one is thinking is a serious thing, if it is the buying of a clock one is very much liking and everybody is thinking it an ugly or a foolish one and the one wanting it has for it a serious feeling and no one can think that one is buying it for anything but as doing a funny thing.

The important thing now to be discussing is concrete and abstract aspiration, concrete and generalized action in many men and women of very many kinds of them and now there will be a beginning of discussing the feeling in each one of being a bad one, of being a good one, the relation of aspiration and action, of generalized and concrete aspiration and action.

It happens very often that a man has it in him, that a man does something, that he does it very often, that he does many things, when he is a young one and an older one and an old one. It happens very often that a man does something, that a man has something in him and he does a thing again and again in living. There was a man who was always writing to his daughter that she should not do things that were wrong that would disgrace him, she should not do such things and in every letter that he wrote to her he told her she should not do such things, that he was her father and was giving good moral advice to her and always he wrote to her in every letter that she should not do things that she should not do anything that would disgrace him. He wrote this in every letter he wrote to her, he wrote very nicely to her, he wrote often enough to her and in every letter he wrote to her that she should not do anything that was a disgraceful thing for her to be doing and then once she wrote back to him that he had not any right to write moral things in letters to her, that he had taught her that he had shown her that he had commenced in her the doing the things things that would disgrace her and he had said then when he had begun with her he had said he did it so that when she was older she could take care of herself with those who wished to make her do things that were wicked things and he would teach her and she would be stronger than such girls who had not any way of knowing better, and she wrote this letter and her father got the letter and he was a paralytic always after, it was a shock to him getting such a letter, he kept saying over and over again that his daughter was trying to kill him and now she had done it and at the time he got the letter he was sitting by the fire and he threw the letter in the fire and his wife asked him what was the matter and he said it is Edith she is killing me, what, is she disgracing us said the mother, no said the father, she is killing me and that was all he said then of the matter and he never wrote another letter.

It happens very often that a man has it in him, that a man does something, that he does it very often that he does many things, when he is a young man when he is an old man, when he is an older man. There are then very many men and there is then from the generalized virtue and concrete action that is from the nature of them that might make one think they were hypocrites in living but they are not although certainly there are in living some men wanting to deceive other men but this is not true of this kind of them. One of such of these kind of them had a little boy and this one, the little son wanted to make a collection of butterflies and beetles and it was all exciting to him and it was all arranged then and then the father said to the son you are certain this is not a cruel thing that you are wanting to be doing, killing things to make collections of them, and the son was very disturbed then and they talked about it together the two of them and more and more they talked about it then and then at last the boy was convinced it was a cruel thing and he said he would not do it and his father said the little boy was a noble boy to give up pleasure when it was a cruel one. The boy went to bed then and then the father when he got up in the early morning saw a wonderful beautiful moth in the room and he caught him and he killed him and he pinned him and he woke up his son then and showed it to him and he said to him "see what a good father I am to have caught and killed this one," the boy was all mixed up inside him and then he said he would go on with his collecting and that was all there was then of discussing and this is a little description of something that happened once and it is very interesting.

It happens very often that a man has it in him, that he does things, that he does something, that he does many things when he is a young man and an older man and an old man, that he feels always in a way about everything, that he is a good enough man in living, that he is a very good man.

It happens very often that a man has it in him that he does something and that thing is a concrete acting and no one would ever think that man had done that thing and that man is a good man, and he does it very often.

It is very perplexing the generalized conception which is of virtue in many men and women and the concrete feeling that is not of virtue in them. Some one builds up convictions from some other one, some know then that they do not believe that thing and some do it then because it is a pleasant thing, some do it to please some one, some begin to believe it and then they lose it and they don't say anything, some begin not to believe and then they come when they are older ones to believe what they began with as not believing but saying it to please some one, very many then in very many ways have other ones convictions come to be the determining frame for them, some believing it then, some who are not believing it then, very many who do not know then whether they do or do not believe that thing. There are very many women there are very many men who are always saying if they had their life to live again they would live a different one, they would learn very many things, they would do serious reading. There are very many who always are going to be doing more serious reading, more staying at home of an evening.

Sensitiveness, measure, kinds in men and women, cowardice and courage, kinds of sensitiveness in them, originality and personality in them, generalized and concrete feelings and thinkings and activities in them this is all really very enormously interesting.

There are many ways of thinking, feeling, knowing, believing in many men and women in all there ever are or were or will be of men and women. One once who was a very intelligent active bright well-read fairly well experienced woman thought that what happens every month to all women, she thought it only happened to Plymouth Brethren, women having that religion. She was a child of Plymouth Brethren and she thought that what happens to all women every month only happened to Plymouth Brethren women, she was twenty eight years old when she learned that it happened to every kind of woman.

There are a very great many men and women and they are very well educated intelligent ones who are very certain that a river can not flow north because water can never be going up hill in a natural way of flowing. They are very certain of this thing and when one understands it about them, some of them, it is astonishing that they can really be thinking such a thing and sometimes it takes almost a quarrelling to make them realize that a river can flow north and that north is not going up hill. They are knowing then that north is not going up hill when they think of it as traveling, they think of north as up hill when they think of it as water flowing and this is very common.

Dead is dead. To be dead is to be really dead said one man and there are very many men who really feel this in them, to be dead is to be really dead and that is the end of them. Dead is dead yes dead is really dead yes to be dead is to be really dead yes, to be dead is to be really dead and that is the real ending of them yes, but still, yes to be dead is to be dead, to be really dead yes, and yet always there is religion always existing and it is better to have everything, to be dead is to be dead some men are feeling knowing thinking believing in them, very many men are feeling thinking knowing believing it in them and some of them some of such of them have it in them that they know that religion is always existing, dead is dead, that they know pretty entirely completely really in them yes dead is dead they really know that in them, religion always is existing, dead is dead yes that is true then, and then they go on in living always doing their religion. To some having this equilibration, this generalized conception is only sentimental in them, in some it is a way of being important to themselves inside them to make it strongly in them this generalized conception in them, to very many it is a very simple thing of being like every one for every one to mostly any one is like this in their living is being of a conviction that dead is not really dead, that good is progressing, that every one is a good one in some way of endeavoring.

Some then and these are now another kind of them from any I have been describing, some then have an ideal in them and always they poetically, romantically, dramatically, idealistically, sentimentally conceive themselves as doing that thing and they are not good at inventing and they are always doing everything and they leave out mostly everything in telling anything and they are always then very fond of telling this thing and so they have it in them to be idealistically, romantically, sentimentally, dramatically one thing and that is always in them an ideal thing.

This happens very often with very many in loving, they are explaining that with that last one they were not real in loving, this they are now doing is really loving, always before they have not been really loving that is certain, this is very common in loving, it is very common very often in women, it is very common it is very often in men in their real feeling, in their real thinking, it is very common in men and women it is very common in loving in women and in men it is very common in loving often in men and women.

Another form of having virtuous feeling is thinking what any one is doing is only a habit in them, and this is pretty common in men, quite common in men and in women. This way of feeling then is that not any one is really a bad one that is hardly any one, mostly every one does a thing because it is a habit and all that they need then is to change their habit to some other thing, some other way of doing that thing doing something and that one will be a good one. They are not actually ever changing the habits they have in them neither is any other one they are knowing but that does not affect their conviction that doing bad things is only a habit in themselves and in every one, and this is indeed quite common in men and in women.

Another very common way of having virtuous feeling about oneself inside one is from having always the sense of being oneself inside one and so one oneself doing something does it, a wrong thing, with a different feeling from any other one and so it is not really then a wrong thing. They are themselves inside them, they feel themselves inside them, each one of them and so then the things they are doing are personal things, not mercenary, vulgar things like those the other ones doing the same things are doing. A man painting, a painter exhibiting has such a feeling. A painter was saying that exhibitions are so disgusting because just looking one sees that all the pictures are bad and that is disgusting, one's own pictures are hanging there and one looking at them and realizing that they are bad things knows by remembering how each one of them happened to come to be not a good one and that then makes it alright for there are reasons that one's own pictures are not good ones while all the others they are bad ones and that's all there is to them, there are not reasons to explain them to the feeling of any one looking at them and this is a very common way of having a conviction of virtue in them in a wonderfully large number of men and women.

There are others who build it up in pieces the virtuous being the virtuous feeling in them, slowly they build it up in living, slowly carefully and always they are adding, piece after piece is being added by them to make sometime pretty completely a whole thing and some of these are very good ones indeed in living and some are not such very good ones, but very many of them are very good ones in living.

There are lots more ways of having virtuous feeling in one than these I have been describing. I am keeping them back now from crowding on me, slowly they will come to me and out from me, this has been a description of a few of them and there are lots of them but I have been already describing a good many of them and always I am understanding women and men more and more by listening to them as in repeating it comes out of them the telling by them of how goodness is in them even in those who never are really talking about any such a thing.

All these then that I have been describing all these then all these kinds of them that I have been describing I am thinking as of the resisting kind in men and women, the dependent independent kind of them.

Every one was a whole one in me and now a little every one is in fragments inside me. Mostly not any one now is a whole one inside me. Alfred Hersland is in fragments inside me, I will now begin again and it will be a describing of pieces then, pieces of perhaps a whole one. Perhaps not any one really is a whole one inside them to themselves or to any one. Perhaps each one is in pieces and repeating is coming out of them that is certain but as repeating of pieces in them.

Of the kind of one that Alfred Hersland was in his being they range from very good ones through to pretty bad ones but this is true of every kind there is of men and women. Alfred had it in him to have his being in him so that it was a little passionate in him, not very affectionate in him, not so as to be very good in him, not really ever very bad in him, sometimes as aspiration in him, more or less as ambitious in him, sometimes as virtuous and didactic in him.

I am thinking now of six of them that have such a kind of nature in them like that in Alfred Hersland and these have it very differently in them than he had it in him and then there was his grandfather Mr. Hissen of whom I have written. There was one and he was not very successful not very not successful, he was successful enough in living and he had it in him to be impersonal and just and kindly enough with mostly every one, and he had not any engulfing passionate nature in him, not at all any such a kind of this kind of being in him, and he was almost altogether certain that to be dead was to be really a dead one and he did not altogether completely like it such a feeling and he could be a little not certain of it inside him though mostly altogether he was certain that to be dead is to be really truly a dead one and he liked it very well that his wife who could be making lively living feeling was very certain that to be dead was not at all to be a dead one and he liked it then that she was such a kind of one and mostly then this one was successful enough in living, and kindly and not meek and not given to aggression and master in his own house by patient overseeing and successful enough in living by patient persisting and this then is all there is now to be written of the living this one had in him.

Another of the six of them was one having it in him to have a good deal in him of the engulfing passionate being of his kind of them but the being in him was not really ever in action, it never amounted to any more in him than to be a little wiggling in him and that was all then, he wanted it to be in action, he wanted to be passionate, and succeeding, and aspiring, and despairing, he tried it always all his living, he was always a little scaring and filling with hope his family for the despair and the possible activity in succeeding in living in him and mostly then nothing ever happened and he came as near in his living as a man can come to failing who is not completely failing in living.

Another one of them had the passionate murky engulfing being in him in a completely concentrated form that made him active, sensitive, amusing and successful, quite successful in living. He was always loving but it never was a trouble to him, he was so active he never was knowing that he was engulfing the other one, that he owned those he needed for loving. He was a very nice, a nice, amusing, sensitive, successful enough one of this kind of them, the passionate engulfing resisting kind of them, in this one this being was quite a concentrated pleasant thing.

Another one had it in him to be completely certain in all his acting and his feeling and his living that to be dead is to be a dead one and so this one must keep on being a live one and must have everything he can be seizing to keep by him and always this one in his talking and his thinking and his feeling was very certain that he was very certain that to be dead was not to be a dead one and if it were, what then, a really noble man would not let it effect him and he was most certainly such a one. This one had some aggression of resisting being in him, this one was quite successful enough in living.

This one that I am now beginning describing had murky passionate resisting being but its action in him was very intermittent and it was at different times in very different conditions in him. Sometimes it was in him in a fairly concentrated condition and it made of him some one very quick and sensitive and charming and a musician, sometimes it was very quiet in him and then sometimes it burst out as uncontrollable temper in him. Twice in his life it led to loving and both times then it made trouble for him for he was not strong enough in persisting to be able to keep on owning the ones he needed for loving. This one was not very successful in living.

This one was very successful in living, this one that I am now beginning describing. This one had this being not at all as murky not at all as engulfing, he had it in him as efficient emotion, as active practical reasonably aggressive resistant action, as steadily and not too sensitively in him, as warmly affectionate and rationally self-understanding. He was a little sentimental and this was all the weakness there was in him.

As I was saying of the kind of being there is in Alfred Hersland there is every kind of variation. To begin again then, to begin now with him, to begin now again trying to describe him as a quite young one, as beginning in his living.

Alfred Hersland, Alfy as every one then called him was as a young one of the living of poor people living in small houses in a part of Gossols where the Herslands were the only rich people living. He was doing all his daily living with the children and the women and the men living in small houses in that part of Gossols where the Herslands were the only rich people living. The Herslands were rich people of rich american living as the natural way of living. In a way Alfred had never had any real experiencing of this kind of way of living, he really did not know very much of any one who was living this kind of living, sometimes some with their children came to see the Herslands and then the Hersland children had to play and talk with these then these children living the rich american living, and the Hersland children mostly were not interested in them, Alfred had not any liking for them, he liked to have all the fruit picked even before it was quite ripe before it was really ready for picking so that those children who were coming to visit them should not be using their trees to pick fruit and enjoy it. Once when some of them were coming, Alfred with David and Martha to help picked all the fruit although most of it was green then, it was mostly cherries just then, picked it all every bit of it and put it in the barn to ripen and he did this so that the children coming to visit

them should not be climbing the trees and helping themselves as if it were an orchard of their own. He had in
him not any disliking for the rich american living but he
did not want the children of that living to make themselves too much at home in his garden in his orchard
with the flowers and the fruit that was part of his daily
living.

Alfred Hersland was a boy and living then with for
him poor people, children, men and women. When he
was a boy, when he was beginning his living he lived his
daily life then doing everything he did then with the
boys the women and men living near him. He did his
roller skating, a little shooting, some camping, a good
deal of fishing, some going about the country selling fruit
he had been picking with them in the orchard in the ten
acre place where the Herslands were living and any other
fruit belonging to any of them that they could use for
selling, he did everything in his daily living with them,
he was with them when they were with girls then and he
did with the girls everything a boy does with when he is
with them. He had then public school living.

There were then the Banks boys who lived near him,
there were three of them, it was the oldest one who was
mostly with him, the second one George who had lost
two fingers from a sickness he had that no one ever
mentioned to him was the one with whom David
Hersland later did his living. The oldest Banks brother
Albert, who later in his living did shoemaking, George
later was a clerk and pretty successful in living, the third
brother then a very red faced freckled one who could crow

very well and always was on fences doing this thing and his later living came when the Herslands did not any longer any of them any more know what happened to any one in that part of Gossols and so there is not to be any telling of his future living, Albert was a good deal in these days with Alfred Hersland and then he began shoemaking and he was not very good at learning at school and once he had a furious anger in him there and he scared every one in the school by drawing a pistol although it was an empty one and he was told not to come any more and he then began learning shoemaking but he was a good fellow to be with for any one and pleasant enough and he and Alfred did everything together then until the shoemaking began and then he went with men and Alfred was not so completely with him then.

There were a number of little houses in this part of Gossols and Alfred knew a good many of the people living in them. Once there was a family that stayed one year there and there were two children an older boy and a very young one, the older one Louis Champion was very much with Alfred then, the little brother was a nuisance to them, Alfred did a good deal of roller skating, some camping out and more or less fishing with Louis Champion. Louis was a pleasant fellow and good-looking.

Alfy was often out in the evening, in the summer he was out a long time almost every evening. Albert Banks was often playing, going about with him of an evening. Frank and Will Roddy often were with them all in the evening. Frank Roddy later in his living went into the country to earn his living. Will Roddy later went into a cigar stand, clerking, and then his father died and he had a little money and he came to be a partner and then he and the other one failed and they were not fair then they very much favored one creditor, they had some trouble, later very many years later some of the Herslands happened to hear from some one that Will Roddy was in jail because of something he had been doing. He was a little fellow and very quick.

So then Alfy and Albert Banks and the Roddy boys were often playing hide and go seek in the summer in the evening. They were very often together in a vacant lot playing or hanging around together somewhere and often enough they would be chasing around in the Hersland orchard and garden. Sometimes there some girls would be with them. Sometimes then Martha Hersland would be with them. Alfred and David very often were playing hide and go seek with Albert Banks and the Roddy boys and sometimes some others, in the Hersland orchard and garden. Sometimes some girls would be with them, sometimes then Martha Hersland would be with them. Sometimes Alfy would make Martha go in. He was then a little beginning to have in him the feeling that he was a good citizen, that he was the oldest son, he did not know then very specifically why she should go in, they neither of them knew very specifically why she should not be playing hide and go seek in the evening but Alfy was beginning then to have such a feeling about himself in him that he should send her in and later then if she did not do something he wanted she should be doing he

165

always said he would then tell his father she had been playing hide and go seek in the evening and then she always had a sullen fear inside her. Neither of them then as I was saying knew very specifically what they were meaning.

Alfred all his younger living was out very often in the evening, then and later in his Gossols living he was often out in the evening, in the summer he was out a long time almost always in the evening. Mostly he stayed entirely in that part of Gossols where he was living. There were some whom he knew who were living in another part of Gossols and he sometimes saw them, sometimes he saw them very often. The Fishers one of these families then were friends of the woman who lived near the Herslands and did dressmaking sometimes for Mrs. Hersland. Sometimes Mary Fisher came to see the second daughter Cora who was not yet come to be a really pretty one. Sometimes Mary Fisher's brother Henry came with her and so the Herslands all of them came to know them and they each one in their way all except Mrs. Hersland came to know the Fishers very well. Mr. Fisher had something to do with horses, that was the way he made a living. Henry went bicycling very often with David Hersland. Mary was the only daughter and all the Hersland family came to know her. Alfred used to stay in her kitchen talking to her. Jim was the oldest son and brother. The Herslands did not, any of them, come to know him. The Fishers were all proud of him, he was a commercial traveler and was apart from them. Slowly it came out about him that he was going to ruin from a taste for

166

liquor. Later he took a cure and was better, none of the Herslands ever saw him, not any of them ever came to know him. Mrs. Fisher was a tall kindly faced kind of woman. She was always good and mostly always in the kitchen. Alfred Hersland was at the Fishers sometimes for an evening. They were not really ever very important in his living.

Another family with whom the Herslands Martha and Alfred and David, never Mr. and Mrs. Hersland, spent an evening were the Henrys and these were not really important to them. They came to know them quite by accident having sat next to them at a theatre one afternoon and then they went to see them. They went there quite often in the evening one or two or all three of the Herslands then. There were four children, James Henry a tall thin one who played the violin while the other ones danced in the evening. Henry a pleasant enough sensible enough fellow to be knowing, Rose Henry a little dark one and Carrie Henry who was just one of them. The Herslands would go there to eat dinner with them, Mrs. Henry browned potatoes, pealed, when she roasted her meat the way french people do them, the Herslands always ate very many of them, the forks and knives the Henrys used for eating were worn down very thin, later then James Henry played and all of them danced pretty solemnly in a quadrille. The Henrys were really not important in the living of any of the Hersland children. Later then they did not see any of them, Mr. Henry later killed himself and every one wondered if he had been crazy when he did this thing.

Alfred played the violin some, he played it very well. He had some musical feeling, he had quite a bit of musical understanding, later in his early Bridgepoint living he was very much interested in playing and in understanding. He made for himself some reputation as an intelligent amateur musician. He came to know then in Bridgepoint in his early living in Bridgepoint a young man who was making music a profession and did some rather nice composing. Later this one gave it up and went into the clothing manufacturing business in which his brother and father needed him, but this is all later history of Alfred Hersland, this all was in his Bridgepoint living, this is now a history of him and a description of the being in him in his Gossols living.

Alfred was neither popular nor very unpopular with those that knew him. He was not pleasant nor unpleasant to any one, he did everything he did with those he was knowing then, he really did with them mostly everything they were doing. To them his future living was not important in him to cut him off at all from them. He was himself inside him, later as I was saying he had some feeling in him that he never had been cut off from rich american living, later then this came to be in him, he still then did everything he did with those he was knowing in Gossols where he was living, not altogether though then, he was beginning knowing some other women and some men, he saw something then of Ida Heard the school teacher this is all to be written later.

Some know more or less of men and women what the being in them are going to be making them do from minute to minute in their living, some have not at all any such knowledge in them of men and women. There are a very great many who are very certain that some one will be doing something and these then have it in them to be easily quickly very completely forgetting all the times they are mistaken. Always then more and more I want to be feeling completely feeling the complete being, all the being in each one I am ever knowing and feeling in them the kind and quality and quantity of work and living and loving in them. I can never have really much feeling of what specifically they will be doing from moment to moment in their living I have not any dramatic imagination for action in them, I only can know about action in them from knowing action they have been doing any of them, I mention this so that every one can be certain I do not know this about any one any men or women, I tell about the living in them from the living they have had in them I cannot ever construct action for them to be doing, I have certainly constructive imagination for being in them, sometimes with very little watching I have pretty complete realization of pretty nearly all the being in them.

To be using a new word in my writing is to me a very difficult thing. Sometimes I am using a new one, sometimes I feel new meanings in an old one, sometimes I like one I am very fond of that one one that has many meanings many ways of being used to make different meanings to every one. Sometimes I like it that different ways of emphasizing can make very different meanings in a phrase or sentence I have made and am rereading. This is a pleasant thing, sometimes I am very well pleased with this thing, very often then I am liking a word that can have many ways of feeling in it, it is really a difficult thing to me to be using a word I have not yet been using in writing. I may know very well the meaning of a word and yet it has not for me completely weight and form and really existing being. There are only a few words and with these mostly always I am writing that have for me completely entirely existing being, in talking I use many more of them of words I am not living but talking is another thing, in talking one can be saying mostly anything, often then I am using many words I never could be using in writing.

Alfred Hersland was of a kind of men and women. Always to me there are kinds in men and women that is certain and now then to begin again describing the kind of one Alfred Hersland is in living, all the kinds there are of that kind of them, all the kinds of ways there are in me of learning them of feeling them.

Some one has milk brought to the house by the milkman and it is wasted and yet always that one is continuing having that amount of milk brought in because that one is thinking that sometime that one will be a sick one and then if the milkman has not the habit of bringing milk every day to that one then when that one is a sick one that one will not have milk brought every day by a milkman. It will be too late then to be beginning then when that one is so sick that one cannot go out to order anything. Such a one can have it that that one never throws away anything, never wastes anything in living and always there is more milk there than that one can be using in the daily living, in a kind of way this is very common, not about milk left, but about a way of feeling in living and a way of acting. Mostly then I have just now a feeling mostly such a one is part of a being. Mostly just now I have a good deal of such feeling that every one is not a whole one that each one is not ever a complete one. One quite young one was loving another one and that one was saying to the one that one was loving, I only love them like you with dark hair and brown eyes for I am a blond one and I could only be loving a dark one. Then this one saw a picture of another one, I could love that one said this one. But that one is a blond one, the one this one was thinking of loving told this one and you just said you could only love a dark one, yes that is true but I think I could love that one, and this is very common, and always there are very many having it always in them that they are a piece of being and always each one is a whole one in the sense that each one is being really in them is existing and sometimes then very often there is to me not any kind of a whole one really in any one and anything and now I am not really caring any more anyway about this thing, about being being a whole one in any one in any way.

It is very hard to know it of any one whether they are lying that is to say it is very hard to know it in any one whether they are knowing the relation between what they are saying and what had happened what is happening to them. It is very difficult to know it of any one whether they, to themselves, are saying what is not what they are thinking. Lying, stupid being in men and women, religion, aspiration, sensitiveness to any one to anything in men and women, appreciation and enthusiasm, emotion and being afraid in them of something of anything of everything of any one, of almost every one, all these then are very interesting in men and women and very often, very very often it is a necessary thing to know all the being every bit of the being in any one to know it of them what they have in them of these things inside them of lying and aspiration and stupid being and virtuous feeling and important feeling and religion and fear and realization of material existing. It is a very difficult thing then to know the being really in mostly every one. Very often when some one is knowing the complete being of some one that one is still only a piece of a being, there is not in the being of that one a quality of completion, there is no reason why that one from the being in that one should keep on existing, should have kept on existing and when that one is a dead one it is an accidental kind of thing that that one should be an ended one, it is not a completed or a cut off thing the ended one, and that is a very common thing to be feeling about many men and women. This is a kind of feeling almost every one knowing him had about Alfred Hersland as I have been saying again and again.

This one that I am now describing was of a kind of one that are very many of them quite successful in living.

Resisting being in them is as it were solid and firm and hard but never aggressive being in them. It is not profoundly sensitive in them, it is as it is in wood when in a tree it is living and then when it is completely useful as a piece of wood to be used for working into a shape for using and it is a solid thing then, an honest thing then, a thing to be adapted for good using, a solid reliable thing then, a completely existing thing then, a thing sensitive in the sense that it repays good handling but not a thing sensitive in the sense that a tree living having living growing being is a sensitive thing. These then that I have been describing have a lack in them, they are complete enough in living, they are each one completely different from every other one, they are themselves inside them but in a true sense they have not in them individual being, they are the very cream of schoolmen the very best thing there can be of any one following a master and working with him. These then are very good men mostly, loyal and earnest and efficient and successful in living. Their working in its resulting is very often a quick and graceful and a little a dull thing.

I am going on describing men and women.

I know one, he is of the resisting kind in men and women and he is completely an instrument being he is so completely that in a sense he has no volition though to very many knowing him he is almost a crazy one in living out ideas he has in him. This one as I am saying and I know very many who know him this one as I am saying is to very many an obstinate exaggerated self directing completely self-directing one and this one is completely an instrument nature, this one is like a violin a completely vibrating thing to anything that can really affect him. This one, I know this one very well in his living, this one in his loving is not loving as mostly men and women are doing who love the attacking kind of them if they are resisting kind of them, the resisting if they are of the attacking kind of them this one as I am saying in his loving is completely loving a resisting one, one like himself and this is very interesting.

Now I will be describing four men, I know them all pretty well, two of them the first and the last are fairly whole ones inside them to mostly every one, the two others are mostly pieces of living to mostly every one knowing them.

The first one has engulfing being so brightly, so gaily, so concentratedly in him that it is a very fresh and gay and juicy thing in him the being in him. He has not much real independence of action this one, he needs some one to start him to do everything excepting dancing and loving, this comes to him from the mere existing of women in the world around him. In mostly everything else some one starts him and he is very gay then in keeping going. When he is a sad one he does not want to see any one, that happens sometimes to him, he cannot start himself then, no one is starting him then, he is a sad one then and not succeeding in living. Always though he is responsible for himself, living gives him that initiative and he goes on living, sometimes he is a little fussy and then he remembers his father was so before him, he would like to be a different person not be like his father in any way and there he is he finds himself being just like his father after all the different kind of living that he has been having.

The second one, I know this one from the history of him from letters he has written, this one has engulfing murky being as hopeful and yet as a weak thing in him. He needs so much stimulating that after he was not any longer a very young one he could not get enough of it to keep going, he never engulfed anything really in his living not himself, not any one not any woman not any man, but he was always hopeful that some time he would do this thing, hope was always there in him, when he was a very young one he was vigorous in aspiring, later he was not vigorous in anything but always hopeful and always of the engulfing resisting kind of them though never really engulfing or resisting anything.

This one the third of these four of them I know very well indeed now and it took me a very long time to know him but that is not what I am now telling. This one was of the engulfing murkily resisting kind of them but he mostly was too ambitious and he had too much vanity in him and was too self-sacrificing for any one to know it of him. He had very much vanity and self-sacrificing and affection and ambition in him and only slowly it came out of him that he was a rather dry engulfing murky resisting being. I like him and I know him I will now tell a little more about him.

Every one is sometime a little a lovely one to me. This is a very nice feeling in me inside me when some one is really a lovely one to me. Mostly everyone pretty nearly every one certainly every one is sometime a little a lovely one to me. This one I am now describing was for some time really a quite lovely one to me. This one was a very gentle one, a very affectionate one, a really very self-devoted one, a really very ambitious one, a really very vain one, a really very appealing one and always also a fairly aspiring one, and always there was murky engulfing in this one but it was a little dry a little very pretty in this one. This one was to very many quite a lovely one. This one's living and being is quite interesting, sometime there will be written a very complete history of this one.

The fourth one of these four men of them that all have it in them to have murky engulfing resisting being was very little to me a lovely one. He was very really a lovely one to his wife and she was older than he was and he really was not a bad one not a good one not a bad one, he was not a very lovely one to most of those he came to know in living. This one was of the engulfing murky resisting kind of them but engulfing was in him the swallowing of very little things, he never had it in him to do any large swallowing, he never was really engulfing a woman he was engulfing, she needed to thrust herself inside him and so he a little was doing swallowing and often he had it in him to be wanting to do to be doing engulfing but he never really knew it in him, he was of the murky resisting engulfing kind of them but he had it in him only really as nibbling.

One having in him very thickly in him murky resisting engulfing being often threatened he would kill himself and he sometimes made a poem before he was ready to kill himself because he could not have in living what he needed to completely content him. This one as a very young one was not a very adroit one, was rather reckless and given to having things happen to him, had courage in him, was a pretty hard one to manage, was quite a funny one. When he was quite a young man he decided on marrying and then when his mother tried to interfere with him he told the people that his mother was a bad one and he told her that he had written a poem and now he would kill himself and she believed him. This one as I am saying was openly a suspicious one, openly a man thinking only of his own well being, he was quite a funny one, he was very popular with men, he was not very interesting to women but they mostly did not at all dislike him, he had been when he was a young one quite reckless and daring, he always had all his living very affectionate ways in him, he always was certain that he would be master in any house which was his own house completely master of it and always he was a pleasant and quite a funny fellow and he could be openly flattering and openly suspicious and he was both all his living and always he was very funny to every one, very amusing, as I was saying he was always pretty popular with men and not at all unpopular with women.

This one of whom I am now going to be giving a very little description is not completely of the engulfing kind of the resisting kind of them, he is a murky passionate resisting one but not a really engulfing one, he is as near to being an engulfing one as one can be without being one. This one is not then a very complete one inside him, that is natural from the being in him. This one then in a way in loving, in religion, loses the feeling after the emotion, must then begin again and this is a natural thing from the nature of him, he is not at all engulfing, he is as near to it as any one can be who completely entirely is not it. I am finding this description very interesting. I am understanding more and more now the being in him. He was quite an elegant one quite a graceful one in his expression, in his daily living, when he was a young one he was quite completely an idealist then, always he had religion and loving in him. This is all I am now going to be saying about him.

I have known several of a kind of them of the resisting engulfing kind of them men and women of this kind, I have known completely some of them this kind of them, I have known absolutely entirely completely one of such of them, I have known pretty entirely completely another of this kind of them, I have known men I have known women of this kind of them of one kind of the engulfing resisting kind in men and women, and these have it that vanity is complete in them, pride is not in them, vanity is complete in them, seizing anything they are thinking they are needing in living is complete in them, elegance is very completely in them, desiring completely successful feeling is completely in them in such of them. They have vanity completely in them so completely in them that they have in them perfectly simplicity in seizing anything they are needing. They have not in them such of them the feeling for the thing itself, they have not love for anything itself, they have in them the needing of seizing distinction, they have in them a complete need of judging for they must always be judging every one as to whether that one has distinction in her or in him. Consequently for them, learning is to teach themselves or have some one teach them to recognize and realize the things that those people realize who have achieved distinction. I am hoping always hoping to be making a complete history of all men and women completely, completely and more completely of them, these then that I have been just describing are connected quite closely connected all of them with the kind that Alfred Hersland is of men and women.

Some men and women are inquisitive about everything, they are always asking, if they see any one with anything they ask what is that thing, what is it you are carrying, what are you going to be doing with that thing, why have you that thing, where did you get that thing, how long will you have that thing, there are very many men and women who want to know about anything and everything, I am such a one, I certainly am such a one. Some when they are hearing any one talking are immediately listening, many would like to know what is in letters others are writing and receiving, a great many quite honest ones are always wanting to know everything, a great many men and women have a good deal suspicion in them about others and this has in them not any very precise meaning. Once this one asked some one he was visiting, just suddenly, — and this door here does that lead into the hall or directly out into the garden, — and that was all he said then about this thing and afterwards every one was thinking he would be using this against them but really then this one was wondering did the door lead to the hall or directly to a garden.

I will describe now very little a very different kind of one from that one I have been just describing. This one as a whole one is like a cannon-ball lying on a bag of cotton, the cannon-ball lying on a bag of cotton as a complete thing was the whole of this one. I am knowing quite well three of these of them, one is more nearly engulfing, one has of him the very largest size in bags of cotton, one and this is the one I am realizing in now describing was a little skimped in the cotton foundation. This is not a funny description, I was not certain I should say anything of the cannon-ball and the cotton, I was almost certain I would not say anything in this description about the cannon-ball and the cotton, it was not to me a natural way of conceiving any one, some one conceived this one as a cannon-ball resting on a bag of cotton, I used that in my description, this is not to me a natural way of talking, I have been using it here as I am saying.

These then that I am now describing are a kind of them that have sensitiveness that is complete suspicion in them, these are of the kind of them that are themselves completely important to themselves inside them, they have resistance in them much less than sensitiveness as suspicion in them. One of such a kind of one once liked very well some one and then that one forgot to give this one five cents that this one had paid for that one and then this one hated that one, had no trust in that one for this one was certain that that one knowing this one was too sensitive to be asking did not think it necessary to pay that one, he never could believe that any one forgot such a thing. Another one once was always certain that some one who one time told him that he would sometime later be successful in teaching meant that he would not be successful in painting and that this was because that one was jealous of this one although that one had just met this one.

Some of these are having their sensitiveness making of them clever, or self-protecting, or sexually wanting anything, without having really emotion from the thing from the sensitiveness in them. Sensitiveness turns into suspicion, cleverness, self-protection, sexual action before it comes as an emotion and these mostly then never have sensitiveness in them leading to emotion by reaction to a person or thing or action. Some as I was saying have it in them to have this kind of reaction I have been describing as sexual emotion and one such a one that I am knowing is quite an interesting one, quite an extraordinary one and sometime I will tell some of the exciting things in her living but not now, now I am going on describing three more kinds of resisting being.

This one is of the resisting kind in men and women, might have been of the engulfing kind of them, was not at all of the engulfing kind of them was only a resisting one, had a feeling of being an engulfing kind of them which made this one have very much emotion of dominating with stern action. This one then is connected with the group I have been describing by this conception she had of her own being but she was different from these I have been describing for she had not the being in her of being something from sensitiveness in her as these have it really in them. In her it was melodrama. Really this one I have been just describing is not so completely clearly in my feeling as I would have them I am describing.

I will now say a little about another one, one who was of the resisting kind of them, not at all of the engulfing kind of them, one who was to herself and to every one always an attacking one. This one was attacking the way a boy is when he is thrown into water and is scared then and every kind of way is hitting the water so as to keep the water from drowning him. Such a boy makes very much splashing. This is the kind of attacking this one had in her living, this one was so scared she was always hitting out in every direction, this one had little moments of knowing she was a timid one, mostly she was certain she was a very attacking successfully attacking one.

I have it in me in being that I am resisting in being, I am fairly slow in action and in feeling, if I am not slow in acting and in feeling and in listening I am not certain that I myself am doing that acting listening feeling, I would be thinking something was happening, it would be over and I would not be realizing that I myself was listening, feeling, acting. I want sometime to be completely understanding every one so that sometime I will be right about every one. And now I am not knowing anything at all really of the feeling any one has in them when they are between fourteen and eighteen. I certainly will be needing to know this thing. I know now I do not know at all the feeling in such of them, those being at that time of living, I cannot then really be right about every one yet, that is certain. I am hoping sometime to be right about every one, about everything. Perhaps I am right now about some. Perhaps I am right about almost all of them. Always when I am not right something is wrong. Sometime I want to be right about every one. I want sometime to write a history of every one, of every kind there is of men and women. I want sometime to be sure when I know something that I am completely right in my certain feeling. Really to be just dead is to be to me a really dead one. To be completely right, completely certain is to be in me universal in my feeling, to be like the earth complete and fructifying.

But all this is one thing and now being in Alfred Hersland is something. Alfred Hersland had resisting engulfing being in him. He knew at this time as I was saying Olga who was Ida the sister of the first governess the Herslands had had living with them, Ida was then a school teacher, Alfred laughed at her, he liked her, there was not much history of this liking for her. Sometimes Alfred saw a good deal of her, once her wrote her a real love letter. As I was saying he knew a good many then, he was doing with them what he was doing then in his living, he knew a good many then and he was doing in his living with them what they were doing in their living then. Sometimes he was quite a little with Madeleine Wyman's brother and younger sister but not enough to be really different in him from knowing any other one in his living. There was young living in him, there was his being inside him, he lived the living of those he was then knowing and soon then he went to Bridgepoint to begin his middle living.

The Hissen relatives were glad to see him, it was very pleasant for them to see one of their sister's children, and to know really that the Gossols living was existing, really existing. They were pleasant cheerful quickly curious and always a little doubting and it was pleasant for them to see Alfred and to feel him and to ask him how his mother was and to hear him and to see that though he was a fairly tall one he looked a little like them and was very pleasant in liking them. The Hersland relatives too saw him and for a while he lived with his aunt and she was interested in him but it was not such a pleasant thing in her and at first he was very much with the Hissen men and women and he was a little tender with them.

It was very pleasant being in this Bridgepoint living, it was very pleasant to him to be seeing, as it is to Gossols' children, many relatives who knew him and had seen him when he was a baby and were thinking then in seeing him of his father and his mother and he was in them the only one, and it was very pleasant for him as it is for Gossols' children to hear the thunder cracking and the lightning shooting and the leaves piling up and then snow coming looking white and then dirty when he was looking up to see it falling and then it was pleasant for him to see skating and then to see a green spring beginning, it was a pleasant thing like it is to some to hear a koo sounding and to be slowly convinced by some one that it is not a clock but a live bird calling.

Alfred as I was saying when he first came to Bridgepoint living was liking it very much that he was then in pleasant living and then he was a little being in love and that was then almost still pleasant living even though the Hersland aunt with whom he was living was trying to be interfering and was just a little breaking into for him the pleasantness of pleasant living he was having then. The Hissens were a little interfering then, were sometimes having hurt or angry feeling, but that was for him then not a part of not pleasant living. He had some loving in him then, he had some tender feeling in him then, he was liking music very well then, he had pleasant living in him then, he had aspiring in him then but it was not yet come to be in him as something that was to be an active thing in him to make living for him in him.

Alfred of course in his feeling loving was feeling it differently in him at Bridgepoint than he had felt loving when he was in Gossols. In the beginning living he was interesting to some as realizing musical meaning, and mostly then he was pleasantly young and quite tall and always giving romantically scientifically restrained superior information and playing the violin not very well but always able then to be directing the one playing with him. There were then women and men who liked him, not enough to make it very different in him from those he had been loving in his early living, but he was a little older now and soon he was quite a good deal older and he had been really loving then and he had been assisted in not loving by his aunt Hilda Hissen who did this very nicely for him to herself then and to him and he was ready then soon to be one who was to be impressive to Julia Dehning as I was very long ago saying. This then was the beginning of middle living in Alfred Hersland. This was then the complete beginning of middle living in Alfred Hersland.

Some have very pleasant living when they are very young men and women, some have anything but pleasant living in them then. Very many have quite pleasant living in them then and when they are writing it then in diaries and letters to themselves and others there is not very much pleasant living in them then. It is a pretty difficult thing to be remembering, in a way ever to be certain about whether one is having, has been having pleasant living. As I was saying Alfred Hersland in his early Bridgepoint living had quite completely pleasant living. I am almost certain. Later then living was exciting and interesting and gay and varied and absorbing and perplexing and sometimes disconcerting and sometimes uneasy in him but it was never again I am thinking quite so pleasant in him. Perhaps it was pleasant in him in his later living, it is very hard to be certain about any one about pleasant living in them, a very difficult thing indeed to be certain about this in any one at any time in the living any one has in them. Certainly his early Bridgepoint living was pleasant in him. This is quite reasonably certain. Later he was not remembering this early pleasant Bridgepoint living. It was not important in him. Really nothing was important in him until his first loving. It was his wanting to stop studying to be marrying and his then slowly not wanting that this one should have him that was important to him. He soon was forgetting his loving this one, he never was really forgetting having been wanting stopping studying and beginning working at anything so that he could be married then. He never really forgot stopping wanting to be married to this one. Not that that was really very exciting but it was important to him, more important than anything that he ever had had in his living. Later he was older and was beginning to know Julia Dehning.

He always had his own being in him, he was always himself inside him. This was always true in him. Sometimes he was himself to himself inside him, sometimes he was not so much himself to himself inside him.

It is a queer thing to me who am really entirely loving repeating that mostly not any one is seeing feeling hearing themselves as doing repeating. Perhaps it would not be pleasant to most of them, indeed very many of them are quite certain they do not at all love repeating. So then a very great many never can come to be realizing what can and what really cannot come out of them. As I am saying very many a very great many are always beginning having a completely new thing coming out of them to themselves inside them or waiting to have something coming so completely out of them that it is really in that quality of being a complete thing to be a new thing to be coming out of them, and this is very common. Each one has their own being in them, each one is of a kind in men and women.

Every one is always knowing the reason why they themselves are failing in succeeding. Each one is knowing certainly each time why he is not succeeding in living. Each one is always knowing why she is succeeding in failing. Each one then has their own steady complete reason for each time of not succeeding. To themselves each one it is a specific thing each reason each time of failing to be succeeding, to mostly every other one sometime the reason each one is giving for each time of failing is repeating a completely feeble one. Repeating and repeating and repeating and beginning and ending and being a young one and then an older one and then an old one and then not any longer a one one; I am sometimes inside and sometimes including this realizing.

Alfred Dehning married Julia Dehning. They were not successful in their married living, this is to be now a complete history of them and of every one connected with either of them.

Alfred Hersland had aspiring in him to be completely full up with something. Julia Dehning had very much excitement in being an interested one. They both of them were not failing in a way in the whole of their living each one, they not either of them were really succeeding in their being either of them.

Loving is a thing a great many are doing. Marrying is a thing a great many are doing. Loving is a thing each one is sometime doing in a way natural to them to be doing. A very great many have very many prejudices concerning loving, more perhaps even than about eating and drinking. I have different ways of having loving feeling in me I am certain; I am loving just now very much all loving. I am realizing just now with lightness and delight and conviction and acquiescing and curious feeling all the ways anybody can be having loving feeling.

Some are never really knowing how much or how little they can be loving. They are looking at some one they are loving and they are thinking they are not really completely loving they could very easily be forgetting the one they are loving, and then they are completely full up then with loving, and they never at any time can be realizing that really they are loving more or may be less than they are thinking they are loving.

Some say alright all but one way of loving, another says alright all but another way of loving, some say not very many kinds of loving are right loving, some say all ways of loving are really ways of having loving feeling. I like mostly all the ways any one can have of having loving feeling in them.

Alfred Hersland as almost any one can tell now by remembering was of the resisting engulfing kind in men and women, not a very complete one in being, fairly aspiring in being and in living, not really failing not really succeeding in the whole of the living in him, not completely certain that to be dead was to be really a dead one, not quite completely entirely utterly certain that to be dead was not to be really a dead one. Julia Dehning was of the kind of attacking kind who mostly are spending their living resisting being at bottom changing in their way of doing any attacking. She was to mostly every one a completely honest one. She had real courage in her, that is certain. She had sweetness in her that is certain. She had stupid being in her that is certain.

The Dehning family as I was saying were living quite completely pleasantly very rich right american living. They were living this in a free way, in a quite generous way, in a completely pleasant way in a fairly energetic way, in a quite successful way, in a fairly gay way, in a quite spirited way, in a fairly peaceful way, in not an ambitious way, in a quite fairly simple way, in a quite thoroughly completely easily pleasant fairly happy reasonably contenting and contented way.

Family living is a thing a family in a way is realizing. Sometimes it is a very funny thing when some are explaining a family living, sometimes it is a foolish thing, sometimes an irritating thing, very often a quite tedious thing. Family living is a peculiar thing because not any one, mostly, is deciding family living and always each one is himself or herself inside her or him and family living is in a way a combination that in a way is not coming from any one. Sometimes it is coming from some one, sometimes it is a combination thing, sometimes it just happens to be existing.

It is a very difficult thing, for very many, to keep on being one liking to be hearing about what another one in the family is liking in living. In the Dehning family living they kept on all of them for a really very long time of living being ready to be listening to what each one liked in living, needed in living, had in living. Dehning family living as I was saying was quite completely a long time a quite pleasant thing. Julia was not really perhaps listening enough to Mrs. Dehning having living to make it later a completely pleasant living but Julia was

191

listening to all the other ones and all the other ones could listen to all the other ones telling about living in them and so really Dehning family living was really pretty nearly a completely pleasant thing.

It is very hard for any one to tell in any other one how much that one is loving another one. It is very difficult to tell it about any one how much loving they can have they do have in them.

Julia Dehning and Alfred Hersland then when they were marrying each other did certainly have loving in them each one of them for the other one. They did certainly come to marrying. They did certainly succeed in not succeeding in their married living.

It is very difficult in quarrelling to be certain in either one what the other one is remembering. It is very often astonishing to each one quarrelling to find out what the other one was remembering for quarrelling. Mostly in quarrelling not any one is finding out what the other one is remembering for quarrelling, what the other one is remembering from quarrelling.

Julia and Alfred and Dehning family living and loving and learning and quarrelling.

Julia Dehning as I was saying was all her living after she was herself to herself in living wanting to be creating living in learning everything in daily living, furnishing, dress-making, decoration, cleaning herself and everything, resting, reading, being a good one, being a useful one. She was doing this then and she came to loving Alfred Hersland. She had loving being in her, she had Dehning family living in her. She was one that to herself and mostly every one was completely living for honest living, for learning living, for Dehning family living. Really she was not learning anything in living, really she could never have the last courage of knowing that sometime she was not honest in living, really she was needing loving and support in Dehning family living.

Alfred Hersland had aspiration in living, had an aspiration to be succeeding. Julia Dehning had aspiration in living, had aspiration in being one learning and to be then completely living. They were married then and they did not succeed in their married living together then.

Julia Dehning and Alfred Hersland were married and commenced being together for all their daily living. Mr. Dehning was then fairly slowly quite certain that Alfred Hersland was not such a reasonably honest one as Mr. Dehning needed for business living. Julia Hersland had come fairly quickly to be certain that Alfred Hersland was not the kind of one she needed for fairly honest daily living, Alfred Hersland was really not failing then, really not succeeding then in living, Alfred Hersland had then important feeling for being one aspiring to succeeding in living. Alfred Hersland had been a young man having it in him that not anything had been in living really important to make for him aspiration to be one succeeding. He had come then to have really aspiration in him for succeeding in being important in succeeding. He had as I was saying all his living some loving feeling in him.

I regret that I do not know completely loving being in every kind there is in men and women. I see some kinds of men and women, I look long at some of these kinds in men and women and I see nothing of the way they do their loving. And then I am very much regretting I do not yet know everything.

Married living was then beginning to be in them in each one of them Julia Hersland and Alfred Hersland and for them in Mr. Dehning and Mrs. Dehning and George and Hortense Dehning. Julia knew she certainly was learning then anything. Mr. Dehning could commence then to have some pride in him in the married living of Alfred and Julia Hersland, he could then have in him beginning to be listening when Alfred Hersland could begin to be talking about doing anything in his living. Mrs. Dehning had then come to have feeling for married living in Mr. and Mrs. Alfred Hersland. She could then fondle him some, Alfred Hersland, and make of him a son-in-law in Dehning family living. Mrs. Dehning then was completely then feeling their married living nicely and with a good deal of active contented feeling which was just then just beginning to be a little commencing in Mr. Dehning. She was not at all then helping Mr. Dehning to this thing, each one then of the two of them had in them their own individual feeling in feeling married living in Julia and Alfred Hersland. Hortense Dehning then was always needing loving Julia in all her living, she Hortense was then a really young girl in her feeling and this in her then could not be at all a thing to be ever then noticed in her by any one. George Dehning was then in Dehning family living, that was all that was in him then in feeling married living in Julia and Alfred Hersland then. As I was saying George

Dehning was living in Dehning family living, certainly he was living in that living then and so he was living in Dehning family living in the beginning married living in Alfred and Julia Hersland and that is enough then about him.

I am beginning to like conversation, I am beginning to like reading some thing about some that I never before found at all interesting. I am beginning to like conversation, I used not to like conversing at all, and social living, and so going on and on I am needing always I am needing something to give me completely successful diversion to give me enough stimulation to keep me completely going on being one going on living. So then I am beginning to like conversation.

As I was saying Alfred Hersland was telling then after he was a married one with a reasonable steadiness in aspiration, with quite a really complete enthusiasm, with eagerness but not with insistence in telling, with quite sufficient pleasure in repeating, with quite a good deal of honesty in hoping, he was telling then what he was needing to be one really succeeding quite well in living.

Mr. Dehning as I was saying was one quite completely succeeding in living, he was one going to be going on in being one being living and always it was more and more important in him in his being that he was listening when some one was telling what that one was going to be doing in living, was going to be needing to be doing what that one was going to be doing in living. So then it was always in Mr. Dehning that he was listening to some one telling what they were going to be doing in living, what they

195

were going to be needing to be going to be doing something. As I am saying Mr. Dehning had in him to be really listening to some one telling such a thing to him.

Now I am thinking of Julia Hersland and Alfred Hersland, now I am thinking of one having really not ambition as emotion, almost not ambition as intention, quite completely ambition as being, now I am thinking of one having completely ambition as aspiration, considerably and hopefully and even enthusiastically and eagerly, ambition as intention, not really ambition as being. This is to be a history of Alfred and Julia Hersland.

Mr. Dehning had come then as I was saying to be doing differently than listening to Alfred Hersland. He gave him a good deal of money as a loan for Alfred to be really then beginning to be succeeding in living.

They certainly did quarrel some all of them. They certainly did quarrel completely some of them. Quarrelling is to me very interesting. Beginning and ending is to me very interesting.

Julia and Alfred Hersland were still living a married living when Mr. Dehning was not going into any house where Alfred Hersland was staying and Mrs. Dehning was still going to see Julia where she was living. Alfred Hersland was then not beginning to be succeeding. He was really not altogether failing.

Mr. Dehning had come to be certain that he could be explaining to any one that Alfred Hersland was not honest enough for daily living, that he could really convince any one of this thing. As I was saying Julia

Hersland very soon after commencing having married living was certain that Alfred Hersland was not an honest one for living, she was certain of this thing, she came at that time then to be to herself completely knowing it as certain that she was an honest one in living an honest one for living, she had always been knowing that Dehning family living was honest enough for any daily living, in daily living.

Alfred Hersland was not believing that not every one was thinking that he was an honest enough one for daily living. He never really was certain that any one excepting Mr. Dehning was really believing that he was not an honest man for any kind of daily living. Julia was certain of this thing that Alfred Hersland was not honest enough for daily living when she came to living in married living. She came very quickly to be very certain that to her then she was one living in her being which was one being complete in honest living and she was soon then coming to be attacking in all her living with this thing. Each one then of the four of them Mr. Dehning, Alfred Hersland, Julia Hersland and Mrs. Dehning had a different feeling in their having reputation of being an honest enough one for living.

Mrs. Dehning was certainly not certain from any being in her that Alfred Hersland was not honest enough for any daily living. She could and did come to be quite certain of this thing. So then she was not certain from any being in her being there to her in her that Alfred Hersland was not honest enough for any daily living. She certainly came to be certain of this thing. So then she was going on talking to Alfred Hersland for quite a long time in daily living and then it came that to hear him or to see him or to know of him made her completely then a nervous one.

The Herslands Alfred and Julia were living married living. They had a baby and it was quite a strong well one but it did not live to be a very old one. It got sick and died of something. This first one was a little boy and Mrs. Dehning thought that he was one looking very much like the father of him. They had later Julia and Alfred another child and this one was a girl and Mrs. Dehning was certain that this one would be in Dehning family living, this one was already looking like the mother of her. Then there was a little boy who was quite a weak little one and about this one it was not quite certain although Mrs. Dehning was pretty nearly certain that he was quite a good deal like the father of him. This one was quite a weak little one in commencing but he came to be quite a strong enough little one a little later in his living.

Alfred Hersland and Julia Hersland went on then for sometime being living. Sometime then they went on being living in married living with each other and then they were not and then they had more living in them and then one and then the other one was ended in being living.

I am thinking now about everything being what it is, everything not being what it is, something being what it is, nothing being what it is, something not being what it

198

is to some, I am thinking of this thing and I am thinking about sense for living in men and women.

I would like to be thinking about some being practical in their being and some not being that thing in their being but I am not just now feeling any understanding of this thing and so I am not thinking about this thing.

In a way being a married one was an interesting thing to Alfred Hersland in a way it was not an interesting thing to him. Being a married one was in a way a very interesting thing to Julia Hersland, in a way it was not a very interesting thing to Julia Hersland. They were married and living then not very successfully to each of them married living. Alfred Hersland then as I was saying was thinking about being one being aspiring in being succeeding in living. Julia was then as I was saying one needing being one having it that she was learning anything. She was completely then when she was doing this thing marrying Alfred Hersland. She liked it a little then and then it went on to come to be quite soon a beginning of a long ending, a long dividing of themselves from living with each other any more in being in living.

Pride and egotism and vanity and ambition and succeeding and failing I like to think about now in each one. I like thinking about pride and egoism and vanity and ambition and failing and succeeding in each one I am knowing because it is very interesting to know these things being in those having these things in them.

Alfred Hersland married Julia Dehning and was then living in married living in a way in Dehning family living. He had then later help from Mr. Dehning so that he could be having what he knew then he was needing to be one succeeding in living. He was not then succeeding in living and Mr. Dehning came then to be certain that Alfred Hersland was one not honest enough for any, for him, daily living. So then there was then married living and having been having children and a father-in-law and a mother-in-law and a brother-in-law and a sister-in-law both quite young ones and a brother then in Alfred Hersland's living and Julia Hersland and not really failing to every one knowing him then and not really beginning being succeeding to himself then and beginning to know some then who came to see him then and not ever seeing Mr. Dehning then but some seeing of Mrs. Dehning then and some seeing of George Dehning then and some living then in the house with him of his brother David Hersland who was studying in Bridgepoint just then. He came later in his living to know other ones and as I was saying he was not in his living succeeding or failing. He knew very well in all of his living Patrick Moore, and later Minnie Mason. Later he married Minnie Mason.

Julia came then later to be really completely separated from him, she came then to be going on being living, she might have then come to be marrying some one, she did not then come to be marrying any one, that was in a way an accidental thing, she might have come then to be marrying one, she did not then marry that one, she went on certainly being one going on being living, she was succeeding well enough then in going on being living, she had children as I have been saying.

Patrick Moore was one in a way succeeding very well in living. Mackinly Young was knowing him then but that was because Young was knowing Moore a little and was going to be a musician. Then there was James Flint who knew Alfred Hersland quite well and then knew Julia Hersland and then knew David Hersland very well and he knew Minnie Mason very well and Alfred Hersland met her then. James Flint always more or less all his living knew Moore and he knew David Hersland as long as David was living, not seeing him very often but always knowing him.

Mackinly Young knew Moore a little. Young was a musician, he was certainly serious in that profession, he certainly was serious in going to be one going to be making something important in musical composition. Young was one who had it in him to be one always steadily working, having certainly real feeling in being one certainly seriously going to be going to do something that would be certain to be a good thing. He was one seeing with his thinking, feeling in his working that everything he was learning was really something and each day in his living he was really learning something. He was one steadily learning more and more and always then when he was composing the only thing that was anything were things that really were not anything, were just suggestions of there being somewhere inside that one a sense really in being living. He was one always working and really then he could do that thing he certainly had been learning but then that was not creation. And yet sense for living was in him but it was a thing to rise slowly in him so slowly that it almost stopped and went so slowly like molasses very thick that not anything he could be learning could be helping him with this thing.

Patrick Moore was not a musician but he liked it that his friends were good at that thing. He was in business and in a way was a man completely succeeding, excepting when he was very worried because he was a poor man, was a man quite completely for the being and the living in him succeeding in living. His being was completely alive and quite lively inside him and he was one succeeding in living excepting when he was worrying about being a poor man a very poor man sometime in his living and this was a strange thing to be in him to many that knew him. He was never a very poor man but he was very often as is common not a quite rich one. He was one doing real estate business and was one almost every one was liking. He had some understanding of Hersland not continuing to be living with Julia Hersland and loving his children. He had feeling for Alfred Hersland marrying Minnie Mason.

James Flint liked Patrick Moore very well. He admired him. James Flint began his beginning living as a musician, he ended his beginning middle living as a manufacturer of clothing. He was a man certainly succeeding in living and yet not one succeeding well enough to be at all startling. As I was saying Flint and Moore knew each other and Flint had come to know Minnie Mason, Flint was a man a good many came to know in living and Minnie Mason came to know Moore and Young, and Hersland came to know her and some years later a number of years later Alfred Hersland was married to her.

Minnie Mason married Alfred Hersland when he was loving again in his living and they were succeeding well enough in being in married living. They went on being in married living.

Minnie Mason certainly did love very much and very often. She came to loving one and being loved by that one and to marrying that one and marrying then was almost a successful thing for the two of them. She had had come then to almost marrying another one instead of the one she married then and that would have been almost a successful thing in having married living. She came later as I was saying to marrying Alfred Hersland, that was quite a successful thing in having married living. In a way she went on knowing the one she had been married to, in a way she went on knowing every one. Minnie was quite happy in loving one and she married that one and she was quite happy in loving another one and she did not marry that one and she was quite happy in marrying another one and she did marry that one. She had really sense for living as I was saying.

Now as I am saying Julia Hersland, who had been Julia Dehning came to know a good many men and women in her living. She came to know David Hersland brother of her husband Alfred Hersland. She came to know James Cranach and his wife Miriam. She came to know Theodore Summers and to know very well then William Beckling, and she came to know pretty well not so very well because Helen really did not like Julia Hersland in her daily living, she came to know Helen Cooke. Julia came to know Rachel Sherman although Rachel was certain that Helen was right about her feeling about living being in Julia Dehning as some called her then, and then later Rachel married Adolph Herman and then with not any changing in her feeling she was a very dear friend in her feeling and in Julia Hersland's feeling. And Julia had known and then was not any longer knowing Charles Kohler, and then there was Arthur Keller whom in a way every one was quite certain would come to be sometime a brother-in-law to her and then there was one she was certainly needing to be one certainly to be existing as being one certainly teaching some one something, Linder Herne, and then there was the whole family that were relations to her, and then there was Florentine Cranach who was a cousin of James Cranach and then there was Hilda Breslau who might come later to be a sister-in-law to her but who really later married another, Ernest Brakes who was a painter, and then there was Selma Dehning who had married into the Dehning family and then had not any love for any one who was not a Dehning and then there was Ella and Fred and their little baby, Robert Housman who came very often to stay with them the Dehnings and with Mrs. Hersland, and then there was Mrs. Conkling the aunt of Selma Dehning and then there was a cousin of Mrs. Conkling and she had five children and they were all girls and all in a way earning their living and very nice girls in home living and Julia liked going out with them. And then there was a doctor who did not do any practicing

Dr. Florence Arden who was quite an entirely magnificent woman and Julia liked meeting her when she met her at any concert or at any meeting and then there was a very rich man Mr. James Curson and his wife Mrs. Bertha Curson who were extremely delighted to know Mrs. Hersland and Julia Hersland was completely happy in spending some time in the country with them.

Julia in a way certainly was quite an excited one in being one being in living. Julia certainly was one keeping on being in living all her living and then she was a dead one. Julia was in a way in living not a happy one, not an unhappy one, in a way quite a happy one. She came to know a good many men and women in living and a good many men and women came to know her and they, mostly all of them, were succeeding in living and in a way she was one having been succeeding in being living. She came sometime to be a dead one. Many others had come by then to be dead ones. Some had not yet then come to be dead ones. There are very many always living that is certain.

One cousin is dead, another is quite a sick one. That is not so strange as they are then in the middle of their middle living, it is not strange and yet it is certainly something one is not wishing to have happening just then. It is natural that when there are very many of a family living and very many cousins and some aunts and uncles living that sometimes some of them should be sick ones, even that once in a while one of them should come to be a dead one. In a way it is a strange thing because very often for many years not any one in the family connection is a seriously sick one, not any one is ever thinking of any one they are then knowing as any where near to dying. Sometimes it happens that one cousin is quite a sick one, sometimes it happens that all the uncles are dead by then and only two aunts are still living. You never can tell anything certainly about such a thing.

I will not worry any one just now with this thing. This is in me for me and I am certainly not scaring myself with this thing.

Each one gradually in living is realizing how being is in men, how being is in women at different ages in them, each one comes in living to know more differences than just very young living, young living, middle living and old living. Again and again it is a startling thing to some one to be learning pieces of this thing of the way being is at different ages in men and in women. I am just now realizing how old men and how old women mostly are when they are sixty-one. I have learnt a good deal about how being is in men between twenty-three and forty-two. I know a good deal about them when they are very little ones, two and three years old in living, something about them when they are eleven, a very little when they are seventeen almost nothing when they are eighteen and fifteen. I know a very little about them when they are twenty-one. I know that being is very differently in them at different ages in different kinds in men and women. I know some when they are sixty are pretty well worn then and some are dead before they come to be that age in living and some are quite young men and quite young women in eating, sleeping, moving, talking and enjoying, and always then each one is learning in living how being is in each one ever living at different ages in their being living, and I, I am just now being quite an astonished one, finding it quite astonishing to be really realizing being sixty years old and being in living in men and in women.

Alfred Hersland came to be older than sixty in living, Julia came to be a little older in living, Minnie who married Alfred later did not come in living to be sixty before she came to an ending, Mr. Dehning came to be sixty and he was pretty well beginning then to be quite an old man, Mr. Hersland came to be older a good deal older than sixty before he was not any longer one being living, he was when he was sixty in a way then a completely old one, he was then in a way then not at all a completely old one.

Certainly some are loving each other more in living than mostly any one is loving any other one. This was not a thing ever coming to be in Julia Dehning, this was not a thing that ever came to be really in Alfred Hersland. They had loving being sometimes in them each one of them. Almost every one ever knowing either one of them thought of each one of them that they had each one of them sometime loving feeling in them.

It is certainly astonishing to know it of each one what that one has done in being in living in himself inside him, to himself inside him, with other ones, with some other one, to any one, to some one. As I am saying each one ever having been, being in living is doing something in some way, is certain in some way in being in some way being living, is going on in some way being in living, certainly mostly every one. This is enough to say just now about each one of them. I will certainly say this about each one of them again and again. This is the ending of just this way of going on telling about being being in some men and in some women. This is the ending of this way of telling about being having been and being in Alfred Hersland and Julia Dehning.

Any one has come to be a dead one. Any one might be one coming to be almost an old one. Any one might be one coming to be an old one.

All that some one knows about some one is what is true of that one as being one doing what that one is doing when something is happening.

This is not then a completely easy thing because then they are ones being ones then not doing everything and not doing everything very often and certainly then it is not a completely easy thing to be certain that that one is being of a kind of a one completely of a kind of a one, that that one is completely that one of that kind of a one of kinds of men and women.

There are some families and any one can be married in them and some in them are not married and some in them are married and any one of them almost any one of them can have some children and some of them have some children and some of them do not have children and some of them do something, do anything again.

Any one being is one being living. Any one being living in any family living is being one existing in family living. Any family living is existing and any one in any family living is one knowing something of family living being existing.

Some when they are being quite young ones are being ones doing something that is being done again and again by some one in a family living. Some when they are older ones are being ones doing something that is done and done and done again by some one in a family living. Some when they are being old ones are doing then something that is being something that is being done and done in a family living. Some all their lives are doing what is being done and done in a family living.

Any one coming to be an old enough one comes then to be a dead one. Every one coming to be an old enough one comes then to be a dead one. Certainly old ones come to be dead ones. Certainly any one not coming to be a dead one before coming to be an old enough one comes to be an old enough one to come to be a dead one.

The one remembering completely remembering something about each one being in the family living has been completely remembering everything about any one being in the family living, is remembering completely remembering everything about some being in the family living, is completely remembering something about every one being in the family living, will be completely remembering everything about some being in the family living will completely remember something about every one being in the family living. Any one can be certain that some can remember such a thing. Any family living can be one being existing and some can remember something of some such thing.

A Note on the Text

The Making of Americans was written mostly between 1906 and 1908. For years it remained in manuscript, shown only to favored visitors such as Sherwood Anderson and Ernest Hemingway. In 1924 excerpts from the book appeared in the *Transatlantic Review*. In 1925 Maurice Darantiere of Dijon printed 500 copies for Robert McAlmon's Contact Editions, and the following year Albert & Charles Boni imported 100 of these and brought them out in the U.S. under their own imprint. In 1934 Harcourt, Brace and Company issued a version abridged to about one fourth the original length by including or excluding whole paragraphs, and in 1966 Something Else Press issued the only complete edition printed in the U.S. All these editions are out of print, but passages from the book are included in the Random House Modern Library's *Selected Writings of Gertrude Stein*.

The complete text of *The Making of Americans* runs to more than 500,000 mostly repeating and repeating and repeating words. Edmund Wilson confessed he was unable to read it through, and wondered if anybody could. Marianne Moore was reminded of "certain early German engravings in which Adam, Eve, Cain and Abel stand with every known animal wild and domestic, under a large tree, by a river." William Rose Benét labeled it a "perfect imitation of the conversation that went on in that tall tower on the plain of Shinar." Katherine Anne Porter warned that "reading it is ... a sort of permanent occupation. Yet to shorten it would be to mutilate its vitals, and it is a very necessary book."

Readers, those who persevere, do shorten it — eyes skip ahead, you thumb ahead, you put it down and pick it up later, starting somewhere else. Why not?

from The Making of Americans is a culling of sentences from *The Making of Americans*. I tried to make among all the books that might be made from sentences in *The Making of Americans*, the one I most wanted to read myself. (You, you should make your own. Let me repeat that: you, you should make your own.) The rules of the game were only that every sentence should be from *The Making of Americans*, they should be in the same order, and each should mean in this context what it means in that context. I broke the first rule by leaving words or clauses out of about a dozen sentences, because they referred to sentences I wasn't including or because they were just more prolix than I was willing. I kept the second rule. I hope I kept the third — if not it was from stupidity, not cunning.

I often pruned paragraphs and often combined one or two sentences each from two or three paragraphs into one, but most of the paragraphing is Stein's and the larger sub-divisions are also Stein's.

I left out one whole section, a long "history" of the younger David Hersland which comes after the history of Alfred and Julia's marriage and includes no narrative. There are things in it that interest me but they aren't easy to get to. You might wonder what else was skipped, what parts of the story, what events or characters are missing: by and large events and named characters are not what is missing.

In August 1925, after reading proof on her book, Stein wrote to Sherwood Anderson:

"It has been printed in France and lots of people will think many strange things in it as to tenses and persons and adjec-

tives and adverbs and divisions are due to the French composi-
tor's errors but they are not it is quite as I worked at it and
even when I tried to change it well I didn't really try but I
went over it to see if it could go different and I always found
myself forced back into its incorrectnesses so there they stand.
There are some pretty wonderful sentences in it and we know
how fond we both are of sentences. "

I said that I tried to make the book I most wanted to read myself — that's a moving target. The first draft of this book was shorter, but I keep putting things back.

When I referred to all the books that might be made from sentences in *The Making of Americans*, I wasn't thinking of different stories but of one story/memoir/lecture of countless versions. As though every variant of some folk tale, every teller's telling, every phrasing of every time of telling, every repeated telling were riffled together in *The Making* — except that what's being told isn't quite like any folk tale. *The Making of Americans* should only exist in the imagination of Jorge Borges or maybe Italo Calvino, except it contains nothing fantastic, and it's been printed. There *are* some pretty wonderful sentences in it.

— D. Sorensen

Set in Centaur, a typeface designed by Bruce
Rogers and first cut in Chicago, in 1914.

Printed by Maple-Vail on acid free paper.